ECONO CLASH REVIEW #6

ECONO CLASH REVIEW #6

EDITED BY J.D. GRAVES

DOWN & OUT BOOKS

EconoClash Review, an imprint of
Down & Out Books
3959 Van Dyke Road, Suite 265
Lutz, FL 33558
DownAndOutBooks.com

The characters and events in this book are fictitious. Any similarity to real persons, living or dead, is coincidental and not intended by the author.

All Story Art by Duane Crockett
Cover Art: "Amp" by ToeKeen

ISBN: 1-64396-163-2
ISBN-13: 978-1-64396-163-7

THRILL ORDER

WELCOME THRILL SEEKERS

ECR is so thankful that you are here right now with us. You could be doing other things sure, and you will get to them...eventually. And when you do these nine originals will be with you, in the back of your mind bouncing around.

I'm writing this during the great pandemic where COVIDIOTS are going on TV and saying things like, "Yeah this virus is bad and lots of people are dying, but what about the economy? We shouldn't socially isolate, that's too drastic a measure. We need to allow sick people to go back to work so that the stock market can go back up. Hard work through challenges is the American way!"

This is coming from the same mouths who decried "death panels" during the Obama years. The same devout believers in every life being sacred. The same paragons of virtue, who, if ever get the bad luck of stumbling upon a publication such as this, would clutch their pearls in mock outrage and indignation. Now, if we sold more copies—things might be different. These worshippers at the altar of the almighty dollar would happily

1

invite us in, clean our feet, and strip search our wallets in an effort to deem us worthy of breathing their air. These are the things, mother warned you about as she tucked you in at night. You were too pre-occupied with the monster under the bed, to pay much attention.

We live in a special time and place in human history. Where wealthy and powerful people can speak half-truths and out right bold-faced lies and go one-hundred percent unchecked by their followers. Blatantly willing to let your grandma die so they can make another payment on their yachts, or third homes, or trophy wive's breast implants, or pool boy's pharmacy prescriptions, or their lizard god who reigns beneath the sea.

Have no doubt dear Thrill Seekers, these people are MONSTERS.

And just like our cover art this sixer's stories crawl with monsters too. Monsters come in all shapes and sizes: Stetson hooded blow-hards, suave coffin openers, uptight alcoholics afraid of the moon, and psychotic prom queens with itchy trigger fingers. Stay vigilante Thrill Seekers. We shall make it through, as long as we socially distance ourselves from our neighbors and read more books!

Inside these pages you'll find: wheelers, dealers, time travelers, frat bros, catfish, criminals, assassins, ghosts, explorers, and no-good Bartlett's, all who roam with impunity. Looking out solely for themselves and disregarding the suffering of others. What would a monster be without the hero who slays it.

During this time of global crisis, we must all do what we can to fight back against the monsters. You can do your part by remembering what my grandmother always taught me:

2

"If YOU READ it, You Must REVIEW it!"

And:

"When passing under tall buildings, don't look up...
a bird will shit in your eye."

Keep up the good fight!

—J.D. Graves

ECONO
CLASH
review

the

PODCAST

QUALITY
CHEAP
THRILLS

Available on Soundcloud, itunes, stitcher, and YouTube.

Available on Soundcloud, itunes, stitcher, and YouTube.

Available on Soundcloud, itunes, stitcher, and YouTube.

LISTEN UP THRILL SEEKERS!

JESUS CHRIST SUPERSTORE
Daniel Marcus

"It'll be the biggest goddamn Christian-themed super mall in the world," J.T. Stubbs said, balancing his formidable girth on the barstool. His solid gold bolo tie clasp glittered in the dim light of the Plano Comfort Inn lounge. Smoke drifted in lazy eddies above the bar. Bursts of lubricious pedal steel and staccato drum-fills issued from the front of the room as Bobby Ace and the Poker Chips set up for their sound check.

Samudragupta "Sammy" Sharma, looking out of place

in his silk suit, the distinctive odor of deep money surrounding him like a pheromone mist, frowned slightly. He didn't much like this Stubbs fellow ("Call me J.T.—everybody does") but he had a reputation for turning straw into gold on the flimsiest of conceits and Sharma, having just sold Superior Fundamentals, Inc, a Duluth-based truck body manufacturing company, to a consortium of Pakistani investors, was looking for a new tax dodge.

"Can Collin County really support a new Christian-themed super mall? You've got plenty of local retail."

That was an understatement. Since a Plano housewife had claimed to see the face of Jesus in a tuna casserole and posted the picture to Facebook, Bible stores, gun shops, and Left-Behind survivalist gear merchants had sprung up in and around Plano like mushrooms after a spring rain. Sharma thought the Tuna Jesus looked more like Jackson Browne, but the area's propensity for religious nuttery was undeniable.

"Exactly," said Stubbs. "My point exactly. It's all about consolidation. One stop salvation with convenient parking. We'll make it free for the first six months then start charging two bucks an hour."

His eyes glazed as he focused on a distant point beyond the bar mirror. He sighed and shook his head.

"We'll crush those indie sons of bitches like cockroaches. I talked the First Fundamentalist into using the Cineplex for Sunday services. Boy howdy, when we start charging for parking…"

He began ticking off his stubby fingers.

"We got a REI for the survivalists. T.G.I. Fridays'll have a Christian-only rock lineup. My brother-in-law Billy Bob owns the Bed, Bath, and Beyond franchise down in Killeen and he's gonna pop out a new one as soon as we get ink on the deal."

Stubbs lowered his voice, "I asked him to go a little easy on the Bath and Beyond and pump up the Bed, if you know what I mean and I think you do."

He looked down at his fingers, splayed out like the blunt tines of a fork. A gold ring with a ruby setting encircled his middle finger. It looked like a link of chorizo, red and ready to burst.

He raised the index finger of his other hand. "And oh yeah, we're gonna run joint promos with the Six Flags Over Jesus theme park down in Red Bluff. Half off admission if you bring a Bible and a receipt from the Barnes and Noble."

"Sounds like you've thought of everything," Sharma said. "At least until you run out of fingers."

The Poker Chips launched into a lurching, polkacide rendition of "I Walk the Line," effectively drowning out whatever reply Stubbs might have made. The pounding bass induced sympathetic circular-waves in Sharma's cranberry juice. Stubbs' glass was empty, which he sought to remedy immediately.

"Bartender!" shouted Stubbs above the melodious din, waving a meaty hand in the air.

The bartender, a lanky young man wearing a Western shirt, cowboy hat, and handlebar mustache, was deep in conversation with a hooker at the other end of the bar.

"Barkeep!" Stubbs shouted again.

The bartender looked up, frowned, patted his friend on the hand, and ambled over to them.

"Kin I git you."

"Two more of the same," Stubbs said.

Sharma put his hand over his juice glass.

"I'm good," he said.

7

The bartender poured Stubbs a generous shot of Old Crow and retreated as the song ground to a stuttering halt.

Stubbs turned to Sharma.

"What do you think?"

Sharma was silent. This was his favorite part of a deal, the pregnant pause, and he milked it without mercy. Stubbs downed his shot of bourbon and wiped a film of sweat from his forehead.

"I'm in," Sharma said finally. He was excited in spite of the small surge of depression he felt at giving this nimrod what he wanted. "Tentatively. I'm going to want names and vitae of the other investors, and I'll have my due diligence team look over the business plan and whatever architecture drawings you have at this time. If all goes well, you'll have a term sheet in two weeks."

Stubbs was prone on a massage table in the back room of Daisy's Beauty and Nails on Division Street in Plano when his cell phone emitted the sound of a tinny, synthisized calliope playing "All My Exes Live in Texas." His pale body glistened with coconut oil as Mei Ling's tiny hands dug deep into his tender spots. She had just slid aside the towel draped over his gelatinous butt and the good stuff wasn't far off.

"God damn it, this better be good." He lifted his head. "Honey, I gotta take this. Grab my phone and hold it up to my ear, that's a good girl."

"This better be good," he said again, without looking at the caller I.D.

"Stubbs, this is Sharma."

The temperature in the room seemed to drop ten

degrees. Stubbs' enthusiasm for the massage dwindled precipitously. "Hey there. I know why you're calling but it's all good. Construction's going gangbusters again. We had that little problem with the rebar quality but I greased some palms at County and—"

"That's fine, Stubbs. I'm sure you've got the graft and corruption end of things well in hand. What I'm concerned about is marketing and strategic planning. You know there's a competing effort that just broke ground outside of Houston."

"What, those guys? They don't even have a Tuna Jesus! They—"

"This is not the first rodeo I've attended, Stubbs. We have a head start, but we need a decisive opening, something really big. I want their investors skittish and desperate. If I can buy them out at a lowball valuation early in the game, we'll have a lock on the religious-themed megamall market for the entire Southwest. This is the big leagues, Stubbs. Time to swing for the fences."

"Well, sure, but—"

"I want you to meet me at U.T. Austin this afternoon. There's a Cessna waiting for you at the Plano airport."

"Austin?" Stubbs avoided Austin like vegetarian lasagna. He regarded the place as a fetid swamp, infested with intellectuals and queers.

"I'm sponsoring a project out of the Physics Department," Sharma said. "I think it might be of interest to us."

As Stubbs walked across campus to his meeting with Sharma, he wondered if he'd made a mistake eschewing the benefits of higher education in favor of alcohol, cocaine, No Limit Texas Hold-Em, and Catholic girls. It was late spring, muggy as a bog, and the campus was crawling with young, nubile women sporting plenty of skin. As a middle-aged, corpulent redneck, he was effectively invisible to anyone under twenty-five and he could ogle with impunity.

The Physics Department was located in Robert Lee Moore Hall, a minimalist 12-story phallus towering over the technology ghetto on the North end of campus. It looked more like a Holiday Inn than any kind of "hall." Sharma was waiting for him at the front entrance. He was wearing white, linen slacks and a navy-blue polo shirt. The crushing heat seemed to bother him not at all.

"Let's go," he said. "You're late."

He led Stubbs though a warren of hallways, through a heavy, unmarked door, and down three flights of stairs. The air grew noticeably cooler as they descended.

The bottom landing was illuminated by a bare, twenty-five-watt bulb. On the far wall, someone had painted a squat, hulking creature with a tentacled head and razor-sharp claws, belly pale and flaccid beneath a midriff t-shirt that read NO I WONT FIX YOUR GRAND UNIFIED FIELD THEORY.

Sharma led Stubbs though another maze of hallways. In one room, he saw a student wielding a blowtorch perched atop something that looked like a diving bell. In another room, two students played speed chess surrounded by a litter of half-unpacked boxes of expensive looking electronics gear. Each shouted "Fuck you!" at the other when they slammed their side of the clock.

Finally, they arrived at a large open area in the back of the complex. An incomprehensible array of hardware occupied nearly half of the space, surrounding yet another diving bell. A scruffy, bearded student hunched near the structure applying a soldering gun to a tangle of cables and circuit boards. Several others pecked away at a bank of terminals.

Amidst the clutter stood a middle-aged man in a moth-eaten corduroy jacket. He had the worst haircut Stubbs had ever seen, his skull mottled with what looked like patches of mange, tufts of hair sticking out in all directions. Nevertheless, he had the bearing of a maestro conducting an orchestra. The air was thick with tension. Something was about to happen.

Stubbs stepped forward, ready to start glad-handing. He regarded any gathering as an opportunity to sell somebody something they didn't need. Sharma stopped him with an extended arm. He shook his head, holding an index finger to his pursed lips for emphasis.

Wait, he mouthed silently.

The professor looked at each of his students in turn, then nodded. One of the students at a terminal said, "Okay, here we go. On three. One—."

"Is that on three, or three, then go?" asked an attractive young woman in a BOYS SUCK t-shirt.

"Fuck off, Darla. One, two...*three*."

A deep hum filled the room, almost below the threshold of hearing. The lights dimmed. Sharp pain flared in Stubbs' dental fillings.

The air filled with an ozone reek. A bundle of wires and boxes next to the diving bell sizzled and burst into flame. The bearded student unhurriedly produced a fire extinguisher from somewhere and doused it.

The professor spoke. He had a voice like a television announcer, deep and mellifluous.

"I thought you put the accumulator behind a surge

protector, Barlow. We can't build a new one each time."

"Well, clearly we *can*, because we *are*…" Darla said.

The professor glared at her. She shrugged, "I'm just saying."

"Okay," Barlow said. "Who's hungry?"

He spun a circular locking mechanism and the door swung open. Mist curled around the edges of the frame. The chamber was empty except for a large, flat, grease-stained box. The students flocked to it like roaches to a discarded donut.

The professor turned to Sharma and Stubbs.

"Sammy," he said."Glad you could come."

He looked dubiously at Stubbs. Before Sharma could make an introduction, Stubbs stepped forward, holding his hand out

"Stubbs," he said. "Call me J.T. Everybody does."

"I'm sure they do," the professor said, taking his hand for a brief moment then dropping it like a hot biscuit.

"This is Dr. Peskin," Sharma said. "His lab, his students."

The students were clustered around the diving bell, gorging themselves on wedges of gooey, dripping pizza.

Stubbs looked at Sharma. Sharma looked back with a slight smile.

Figure it out, he seemed to be saying.

"So what's that contraption," Stubbs asked. "Some kind of fancy pizza oven?"

Peskin chuckled. "Not exactly. That isn't just any pizza. It's an extra-large jalapeño jack chorizo pizza from Ernesto's on the south side of campus. Something of a local legend, actually."

Stubbs's beady eyes widened. "You mean it's some kinda transporter deal, like Star Trek?"

Peskin turned to Sharma. "He's not as stupid as he looks, is he?"

"He has a certain naive cunning," Sharma said.

Peskin looked back at Stubbs. "No, not at all. The thing is, Ernesto's burned to the ground last year. Ernesto himself is currently serving four years at Huntsville for insurance fraud and arson."

Stubbs looked at Peskin, at Sharma, back at Peskin.

"Nuh-uh," he said. "No way. A time machine? Boy howdy, you got yourself a time machine?"

Peskin shook his head. "Not bad, but...no. Time travel is impossible. Entropy, second law, and all that."

Stubbs nodded. He patted his jacket pocket. "You mind if I smoke in here?"

"I'll break your arm if you do," Peskin said mildly.

Stubbs shrugged. He was used to a constant low level of hostility from pretty much everyone he met.

"Okay, I give up. What is it then?"

Peskin pushed his hands together in a steeple. He appeared to be collecting his thoughts.

While they were talking, the students had drifted over from their feeding frenzy.

Stubbs turned to Darla. "Honey, you think you could scare me up a beer, that's a good girl."

"Bite my ass, fat boy," she said cheerfully.

The other students snickered. Sharma tried to contain a smile. Peskin ignored the exchange.

"Our universe is just one of many," he said. "If the meta-universe were an ocean, ours would be one of a googleplex of bubbles comprising the foam on its surface. You with me so far?"

"You bet," Stubbs said, thoroughly lost. He elbowed Sharma."Googleplex," he whispered.

Peskin glared briefly, then continued, "The laws of physics are not invariant from one universe to the next. Fundamental constants have different values, elements decay at different rates, even the speed of light is not consistent."

He seemed to be warming to his subject, like a preacher to a particularly juicy manifestation of sin.

"In some of these universes, even the passage of time is different. A million years here could be the blink of an eye there. Now back to our foam, some of these bubbles are very close together, topologically speaking. That is, some of the universes are nearly identical. Minor details might differ. For example, there is a universe identical to ours in all respects except that, there, the Knicks beat the Lakers every time."

Barlow snorted, "Yeah, right. That's off the continuum, Doctor P."

Peskin shrugged, "A singularity is a mathematical abstraction, Barlow."

Barlow nodded sheepishly, "Yeah, I guess."

Some sort of Zen moment had passed between teacher and student, but as far as Stubbs was concerned, they were speaking in Mandarin.

"So, what we're looking for, Stubbs, is a universe identical to ours except that time passes at a different rate. Depending on what we're looking for, we find the universe with the appropriate rate differential, open a portal, and grab what we need."

"Huh," Stubbs said. "So, the extra-large jalapeño jack chorizo pizza—"

"—is from the universe where Ernesto's is eleven months behind ours, figuring from the Big Bang onwards."

Big bang...Stubbs thought of Mei Ling and was lost briefly in fleshy reverie. He pulled himself together.

"So, what you're telling me is, basically, you got yourself a time machine."

Peskin shrugged, "Pretty much."

Stubbs nodded, starting to see the possibilities.

"So tell me, Doc, you ever brought over any people?"

"As a matter of fact we have," Peskin said.

One of the other students, a chunky fellow with a shaved head, Coke bottle glasses, and a tiny soul-patch, spoke up.

"John Lennon," he said. "Art school phase."

Barlow laughed, "What a douche."

"Word," Soul Patch said. "He wouldn't shut up about himself."

"Me auntie toor up me fookin pomes," Darla said, in a passable Cockney lilt.

Soul Patch nodded, "Exactly. We gave him a hundred bucks, my kid brother's Fender Squire, and put him on a bus to Nashville. He'll be fine."

Nobody spoke for a long moment.

"We gonna tell him about Hitler?" Darla asked.

Peskin coughed, "Yes, well...most unfortunate. A favor for a friend in the Psychology Department..."

"...who you were boning at the time," Darla added.

Peskin glared at her, then shrugged, "Indeed. He shaved the moustache, stole some Dockers from the Men's Faculty Locker Room, and took off on his own. We're pretty sure he's the new Director of Consumer Experience at Apple."

Sharma winced.

"Hoo boy," Stubbs said.

He looked at Sharma.

"I'll tell you what, though. This brings up some interesting possibilities for Opening Day."

"It does indeed," Sharma said.

The only people out in the open during a typical Indian summer afternoon in East Texas are drunks, meth dealers, and outlet shoppers. It's so hot you can grill quesadillas on the sidewalk. The humidity induces lizard-brain panic that you're trying to breathe underwater.

On opening day for the Tabernacle Megamall, a heavy sun beat down on eighty acres of substandard concrete and Chinese prefab. In spite of the inhuman conditions, the marketing blitz had attracted a respectable flock of rubes, willing to scuttle from their air-conditioned muscle cars and pickups to the climate controlled mall interior while newly-poured parking lot asphalt threatened to suck the shoes off their feet.

The tantalizing hints about a special guest had been especially effective. Who would it be? Devin Nunes? Ted Nugent? Britney? Speculation was rampant.

Stubbs was waiting for Sharma in the Tabernacle Megamall Security Operations Center. It looked like NASA Ground Control. Banks of monitors covered two walls; the others were floor-to-ceiling two-way mirrors that looked out over the mall's central commons. Half a dozen middle-aged men in Mall Security uniforms muttered into spidery headsets and hunched over keyboards.

Many of the stores had set out booths and displays in the commons. The Gun 'n' Grog had tapped a keg of Lone Star and a gaggle of patrons clustered unsteadily around the Glock table.

Sharma entered the room and walked up to Stubbs,

"Nice crowd."

Stubbs nodded distractedly, "Ayup."

"How's it going with our visitor?" Sharma asked. "I heard he came through kind of late but that's all I know."

"Yeah, the eggheads had some trouble with the gizmo. First try brought back a ton of sand and half a camel. Messy as all get out."

Sharma winced.

"Yeah, you got it. They cleaned everything up and tried again and this time he came through all right. Guy was wearing a filthy burlap toga and smelled like ass. He took one look around and started screaming like a little girl. We tried to get him into a shower and that wigged him out even worse until he got used to it, then we couldn't get him out. We shot him up full of Valium and he's pretty quiet now. Got him into an all-white track suit from the Sport Authority and he's looking pretty sharp. I gotta tell you, in spite of him being a bit skittish and all, there's something about the guy. He's the genuine article all right."

"Glad to hear it, Stubbs. What are we going to do with him in the program?"

"We're gonna keep him pumped full of Valium, welcome him to Texas, do a little meet and greet with the crowd, laying on of hands, that sort of thing, then get him out of there before he starts screaming again."

"Works for me."

They were set up in Theater 6 at the Cineplex—stadium seating, IMAX sound, and a decent backstage area. Stubbs looked out from the wings to a packed house. Baby strollers dotted the aisles. The big room was filled with the white-noise static of many conversations, like a huge swarm of sleepy bees, punctuated by the occasional Texas holler.

Behind the main curtains, a shortish, thin man with shoulder length hair and a hawk-like nose sat hunched on a wooden stool. Next to him, a small table held a glass of water. He seemed calm enough, muttering to himself and glaring at Stubbs from time to time.

Sharma appeared at Stubbs' elbow.

"We ready?"

"Yeah, pretty much," Stubbs nodded to the tech, a pimply teen with five-day head stubble and huge dangling crucifix earrings. "Kill the house lights, open the curtains, then hit the spotlight on cue, just like we practiced. Ready, steady…go."

The theater plunged into darkness. The curtain whispered open. After a chorus of gasps, the house fell silent.

There was a long, pregnant three-count, then the silky, ebullient voice of the announcer filled the room. Stubbs had hired Hurricane Bob, the weather guy from KBUG Houston, for his reassuring coverage of natural disasters.

"And now, the moment you've been waiting for. Here to bless the grand opening of Plano's Tabernacle Megamall, let's give a big Texas welcome to the man with the plan, your favorite carpenter, Jesus Christ!"

A single spotlight beamed down from the ceiling, bathing the seated Jesus in bright, white light. Stubbs had run the house fog machine for two minutes, just enough so that the spotlight beam was a solid bar of illumination, widening slightly from ceiling to floor. It looked like it was shining down directly from Heaven. The track suit was a glowing nimbus.

The crowd seemed stunned. A ripple of applause began, faltered, then caught hold, filling the room.

Jesus stood up and took a sip of water. The house fell silent again. He looked out into the crowd, shielding his eyes, then he began to speak.

His voice was liquid, hypnotizing. Stubbs couldn't understand a single word.

"Guy knows how to work a room, I'll give him that," Stubbs whispered to Sharma. "Sure wish I knew what he was saying."

"You're not telling me you didn't think to get a translator?" Sharma asked.

"How was I supposed to know? The Bible's in English, ain't it?"

Sharma fixed him with a long stare, then shook his head.

"Forget it, Stubbs." He paused, listening. "I think it's Aramaic, which was a Hebrew dialect. It might be close enough to the modern. We have to know what he's saying."

"Jesus talks Jew? Come on, Sammy, you're yankin' my crank here." He took note of Sharma's expression. "No, I guess you're not."

Jesus was becoming more animated, emphasizing his words with sharp hand gestures.

"Well, hold on now," Stubbs said. "I know a Jew, guy over in Houston. Maybe he can help."

He pulled out his cell, scrolled until he found the number, then jabbed the display and held the phone to his ear.

"Hey, Ira? This is J.T. Yeah, Stubbs...No, I'm just fine, how are...Well, hey now, I told you, that's a long-term investment. We gotta line up distribution, marketing...Yeah, like I told your lawyer boy we got at least a two-year horizon…Ayup…ayup."

Stubbs was listening, nodding, then noticed Sharma's glare.

"So hey, Ira, the reason for my call, you talk Jew, right? Yeah, Hebrew, s'what I meant. I got a situation here, and I could use some translating…Yeah, hang on, I'm gonna put you on speaker."

Stubbs held the phone out in the direction of the stage. There was a pause, then Ira's tinny voice issued from the phone.

"Wow," he said. "Wow. Where'd you get this guy? He's hopping mad."

"That don't matter," Stubbs said. "He's a standup act I'm lookin' to invest in. What's he saying?"

"The phrasing is a little weird, and there are some words I don't understand…"

"That's okay, Ira, just give me the ball park."

"Okay…You sons of bitches. You, uh…effing…sons of bitches. Why have you brought me here, you…defilers of camels. I will…ravish…your wives, daughters, and…camels…with my tremendous phallus of…camel. You whores, you painted whores and…malformed…sons of whores…' *It just goes on like that.*"

"Hoo boy," Stubbs said.

"We have to get him out of here," Sharma said. "Thank Ganesh the Plano Zoo giraffe had triplets—that pretty much dominates the local media coverage. Otherwise we'd be crawling with TV crews and we'd be really sunk."

"Thanks, Ira," Stubbs said into the phone. "I'll call you in a couple days about that other thing."

He jabbed the keypad and slipped the phone into his pocket. He turned to the stage crew.

"All right, people, we got ourselves a Code Two. Kick it into gear, right now."

Five seconds later, the house lights went out and the sound cut off. A security team hustled the struggling Jesus off the pitch-dark stage. He shouted a little more, then he went limp and began to sob.

The house lights came back and Hurricane Bob's oily voice filled the room. "Ladies and gentlemen, we've had a small technical problem. We'll be back in just a moment. Thank you for your patience."

Jeers and catcalls issued from the crowd. Stubbs turned to a shadowy figure standing in the wings, "Okay, big fella, you're on."

The man stepped into the light. Standing about six-two, pushing three hundred pounds, he would have been an imposing figure even without the sequined jacket, oversized sunglasses, and jet-black pompadour. He held a vintage Gibson J-200 by the neck. Inlaid mother-of-pearl roses covered the deck of the guitar, throwing rainbow highlights. It looked like a ukulele in his meaty hand. He staggered a bit as he walked forward.

"You okay?" Stubbs asked.

"Ayuh," the man said. "Just threw up a little for a second. I'll be fine."

"All right, then, give 'em hell."

Sharma looked at Stubbs with something resembling respect as the opening bars of "Heartbreak Hotel" reverberated in the auditorium.

"Well done," he said.

Stubbs shrugged, "My daddy was a hard man, Sammy, barely gave me the time of day, and he died drunk in an oil rig fire when I was twelve, but there's one thing he taught me."

21

"What's that?" Sharma asked.

"Always have a backup plan."

In the Tabernacle Megamall Security Operations Center, huddled on a mattress in the back of a detention cell, Jesus wept.

IN JUST THE
RIGHT LIGHT

STORIES BY WILLIAM R. SOLDAN

PARTY BUS
Preston Lang

Steve Hu was still forty miles from the Mexican border when the dudes broke his stripper pole. Dudes always did, and Steve was glad. Now he could keep 300 bucks out of the deposit. It was right there in the PartyBus2000 contract. A new one cost 18.99.

No trouble at the border then the boys played Diplo and tried out broad Mexican accents until they made it to the hotel in San Samuel. They weren't the worst crew Steve ever had. No fights, no tampering with windows or mooning roadside vendors. They waved happily when he dumped them in front of the Fiesta Hotel—*Adios, Party-Bus2000.*

He was done with them until four o'clock on Sunday, so he put the bus in the garage then made it to his hotel, a quieter place, mostly older Americans or tourists from Japan and Germany. He took a shower and went to the bar. Friday night he could drink as hard as he wanted. Sleep all day Saturday. Quiet little dinner. More sleep. Drive the kids home on Sunday.

When Ernesto sat down on the next stool, Steve had trouble figuring out whether or not it upset him.

"I'm going to need your help soon," Ernesto said.

"How much?"

"It's a little different this time. You'll see."

Three men at the far end of the bar were watching TV—close-of-day stock prices from New York. When Steve started working this route, he'd stayed at different hotels where there were few Americans and no Asians. He'd met Ernesto at one of those places. The people were nice but curious about him, and he learned enough Spanish to talk about kung fu, or Morena, or either kind of football. But after a while, that became too tiring, and he just wanted to sit and drink as quietly as possible.

"Are you bringing down any girls soon?" Ernesto asked.

"Why do you want to know that?"

"I want you to bring a girl back up."

"I don't carry anything that can talk."

"These boys with their beer hats? They can't talk?"

"You know what I mean."

"I know what you mean, but it doesn't make any sense. Carrying this girl is safer for you than anything else you've

25

carried. And we'll give you the same rate. 50 kilos of girl. Same as dead weight in a canvas bag."

"I'd carry her in cargo?"

"No. She'll sit with the other girls. They'll text each other, read Babysitter's Club. Whatever young women do on a bus."

Steve carried about four or five times a year. He probably would've gone under already if it weren't for the cushion he got working for Ernesto. And he always told himself if he got busted at the border, he'd just commit suicide before it came to trial. The idea had never seemed that frightening, so there was no reason to turn down this offer except that Steve didn't like to feel he was owned by a crook.

"I don't think so," he said.

"It's not going to be for another few weeks at least. When is the next time you're bringing down girls?"

Steve had an all-female engineering society from Caltech scheduled the next month, but he didn't tell Ernesto.

"How about this: *I* drive the bus back to the states?" Ernesto said. "You bring the girls down, then tell them— *Look at this handsome guy who's taking over.* You still get your money."

"You have a license to drive an American bus?"

"I can drive a bus."

"No."

"Well, I offered."

An offer he knew Steve couldn't accept. Meaningless.

"Can I think about it?"

"I'll let you think about it. But, Steve, we might have to insist on this."

"Please don't threaten me."

Ernesto smiled, paid for the drinks, and left the bar.

Steve went back and watched *Friends* in Spanish, got even more drunk, and threw up all over the bathroom. When housekeeping knocked, he sent her away and cleaned up as best he could with paper napkins and an old tee shirt. He tried to rinse off the little bathroom rug in the shower, but it still smelled. It was silly for him to pretend he was any better than stupid bros who hooted and broke stripper poles.

The ride home was uneventful. Most of the boys were hungover and dozy. A few of them tried to organize their feelings about the local prostitutes and American girls they'd met—were they hoes, skanks, or buffaloes? The border was a breeze—they were so undeniably American. Steve had them home half an hour early, but when he told them he was keeping 300 out of the deposit, one of them got in his face.

"That pole wouldn't hold a fifty-pound stripper," he said.

"Read the contract you signed."

"We're not paying it."

"Take me to court, then."

"That's not a real pole. That's a pole for some third-grade striptease. You did this on purpose. You knew what would happen. Don't try to con us."

He was ready to fight, and Steve didn't care.

"You break something, you pay for it. Or I guess your mom does."

"Talk about my mom? I'm going to ass-fuck *your* mom on yelp."

The kid was a little bigger than average and half his age, but Steve thought he'd do all right if it came to it. Two of the kid's friends pulled him back.

"Dude, it's not worth it." They were laughing.

As he drove off, Steve heard a bottle break on the back of the bus.

On Tuesday, he got two cancelations for the next three weeks. On Wednesday, he saw that the boys had not only voided the deposit fee, but they'd managed to erase the charge for the entire trip. The card had seemed okay when they first put it down, but now all the money was gone. The name and address attached to it were false. Steve had been getting sloppier about verification and backup lately. The name of their fraternity was fake, as were all the names on the ride list. Most of them had played it straight, but maybe Roger Schlongmann jr. should have been a tipoff. This was a funny story for them, a great victory. The best part was that one bro who didn't know what they were pulling and argued with the bus driver about a fee that would never be paid. Hilarious.

The next morning, when he checked the bus, he saw that three of the tires were slashed. It was the cheapest garage he could find, but still—how the hell does that happen? And there was no time to shop around for a good price because he had another group going down on Thursday. He made calls all night Wednesday, but he didn't end up with much of a deal. Bus tires cost, and you can't skimp on them, especially if you do border runs. Steve had to drive 80 miles in his car, haul the things back to the garage and fight with the wheels all morning. Had the boys come in and slashed his tires? Seemed unnecessary after they'd scammed him on the trip, but who else would do this? The garage had 24-hour video, but only one camera was working. Steve watched on fast-forward for half an hour, but then he had to pick up his group.

They were older, mostly in their 40s and 50s, a magical realism book club. They asked Steve where he was from.

"California born and bred."

Easier than telling them his whole story. Flying to America at age five with an auntie he never saw again. Joining a mother he didn't remember. They probably would've listened politely then had a lot to tell him about immigration and sacrifice and motherhood. They played with the stripper pole a bit, but they weren't serious and no one broke it. He dropped them at a timeshare, parked his bus, then went back to his hotel to drink. He knew he had to stay until Ernesto showed. He couldn't play it too desperate, but he needed money. Eight beers in, Ernesto showed.

"You'll take the girl?"

"I need 12 grand."

"That's more than we're paying."

"I've had bus trouble."

"That's your own issue. You've got to take care of your vehicle, Stevie."

Ernesto wasn't obvious, but Steve caught it. It wasn't the boys who'd wrecked his tires.

"I'll take the girl. But I need 12."

"You know I can't authorize a change like that."

"What can you give me?"

"Eight? I think. When are you bringing down girls?"

"Three weeks. On a Tuesday. I think it's their spring break."

"White girls, Black girls?"

"I don't know."

"Sorority?"

"Engineering society from Caltech."

"Yeah," Ernesto said. "I think this will work."

It didn't take Ernesto long to find their picture on his phone. East Asians, white girls, Indians. They'd won some kind of prize recently. Ernesto showed Steve.

"Looks like they found a new way to estimate the weight of Saturn."

"That sounds like a stupid thing to do," Ernesto said. "On the way back, you're dropping them off at their school?"

"That's right."

"You'll drop my girl on their campus. Someone will pick her up straight from your bus."

"Who is she?"

"Her English is okay. She won't want to talk to you much."

"What do I call her?"

"Sophia, probably. Tell the other girls to call her Sophia."

Steve had a lighter schedule than normal over the next three weeks. He never found anyone on the garage surveillance video. One night he drunk-called his ex, but she didn't answer. He was glad when the time finally came to take down the Caltech girls. They drank a little on the bus, but they didn't touch the stripper pole—they were engineers. He left them Friday, got drunk that night, then on Saturday, he sat at the outdoor café until Ernesto came by to give him half the money and final instructions. Before sunup on Sunday morning, Steve brought the bus into the hotel lot. Five minutes later, he heard a knock on the door, and he let the girl in.

"Como estes?"

"Fine. I'm fine."

Ernesto was right: she really didn't want to talk to him. She looked about sixteen, but she was probably older. Or maybe she was younger. Steve knew some of these bastards took child brides. Or maybe he didn't know what he was talking about—Sophia could've been a 23-year-old accountant who needed to leave town quietly.

She lay down in the back of the bus, and Steve thought of his own daughter who lived in New York. She was a second grader. Last he heard she was still biting other kids. Sometimes he looked at parenting magazines to see if there was anything about girls growing up without fathers and how that made them bite people.

When dawn came, the lobby manager came out and told him he couldn't park a bus in the lot. There was room for it, but they had their rules. Steve gave him 20 American, and that got them through the shift. Then he had to stall the midday manager until the girls showed up at 1 PM, smiling and wet-haired. They didn't seem to have a problem with Sophia on their bus, but Susan Lim, the point-woman for the trip wanted clarity.

"Sophia is the daughter of a good friend of mine. Needs a ride."

There was a little more traffic getting out of town than usual, but things opened up on the highway. They weren't blasting music, but it was loud enough that he couldn't hear their conversations. From what he could see, Sophia seemed to be doing all right. About 40 minutes from the border, Susan came up front.

"Her name isn't Sophia."

"Naming customs in Latin American cultures—"

"And she's scared."

"She's a little shy around such accomplished women."

"You're going to have to tell me what's happening."

"I think you need to mind your own business."

"I chartered this bus. It is my business."

"You have nothing to worry about."

"I'm talking to you now because I want to help. I want to help everyone. But if you treat me like I'm stupid, you'll regret it."

"Okay. Look. There's no risk for you guys. But Sophia gets a little nervous at the border. Do you understand?"

"Do you think it's right to do this without telling us in advance?"

"Maybe it isn't. I'm sorry."

"You're sorry?"

"I don't know your views on ICE, but I don't think they were particularly fair with her or her family."

"Well, as long as *you* feel all this makes sense."

"How'd your parents get to the states?" Steve asked.

"How do you know they're not American-born."

"Are they?"

"F1 visa for medical school."

"That's great. My mom spent six weeks crammed inside a freighter. So let me be as honest as I can. I think we'll cruise in without a problem. But worst case for you? You'll have to sit in a little hut at the border for a few hours and wait for somebody's dad to pick you up. Think about what a story that will be."

"You didn't have to say that. That last part."

"I'm sorry. I'll leave it up to you, Susan. What should we do?"

Steve knew the guard at the border by face, but still everyone had to get off the bus.

"Good time down south, ladies?" he asked.

The girls nodded and smiled half-heartedly.

"A little beach? A little tequila?"

"It was very pleasant," Susan said.

The guard noticed that four of the girls were wearing Caltech tee shirts. Sophia was one of them.

32

"So you're all geniuses?"

"We work very hard," Susan said.

"All right, let me see passports."

The guard checked them quickly until he came to Sophia.

"What do you study, Sophia?"

"I study mathematics."

"Pi R square? Cake R round? That kind of thing?"

"No."

"Hey, what do I know?"

He handed her the passport.

Back in the bus, into the United States of America. In the mirror, Steve could see that Sophia was holding hands with the girl on either side of her. Thirty miles in, he got a call.

"PartyBus2000, how can I help you?"

"You're the bus driver, right? You're on speakerphone?"

"No, I got the headset on."

"Good, because the next thing I say, only you should hear."

"Go ahead and talk."

Steve spoke quietly, and there was music playing behind him.

"I'm looking at a picture of PartyBus2000 right now. If I have to find you, it'll be really easy. But I think you're going to be smart. I'm going to tell you where to drive. Then we're coming onto the bus to get the girl. Then you get to drive away."

"Why would I do any of that?"

"You want to be a part of this? You know Richie? He was supposed to meet her. He's dead."

"I don't know Richie."

33

The man gave Steve an address.

"I know you can get there in less than an hour."

Steve looked it up. 43 minutes away. Some kind of agricultural storage facility out in the desert.

"You want me to drive there with a bus full of American college girls?"

"Get rid of them."

"Just kick them off the bus?"

"Yes."

"These are USC kids. Their dads own California."

"I don't care. Get rid of them."

"What's Sophia going to think when I tell everyone except her to get off at a gas station?"

"Sophia? Oh, you're calling her Sophia."

"What's her real name?"

"Look, bus driver, you don't want to get hurt. Boot the bitches off your bus then bring me Sophia."

"I'm supposed to hold her in a headlock while the rest of them get off? How do you think that's going to look? College girls take pictures of everything. They'll call police. I don't want that. Do you want that?"

Steve looked behind him once. No one was interested in anything he did.

"You need to do what I tell you."

"I don't care about this girl. But what you're talking about makes no sense. I'll get in trouble, you won't get your girl."

There was silence on the other end for about twenty seconds.

"You got a better idea?"

"I drop the girls off normally, at their school. Sophia thinks she's going to get a call from someone—I'm guessing that's Richie. Maybe half an hour goes by—no Richie,

34

no phone call. She gets nervous, and I tell her I can drive her someplace where she can wait for Richie. Should be easy at that point."

"Somewhere in Los Angeles?"

"That would make the most sense."

"All right. Where are you?"

Steve told him where he'd been 20 minutes earlier.

"Okay, I'm going to have a car on your ass in 10 minutes. Drive straight to school. Dump off the college chicks. I'll have a meeting spot set up by then."

Steve took the next exit and stopped at a gas station. He walked back to Sophia.

"You have to get off this bus now."

"What the hell?" Susan said.

"You need money?" he asked Sophia.

"I have money."

The idea that she'd need a few grimy dollars from a bus driver was disgusting to her.

"You're not throwing her off the bus," Susan said.

"No, I'm not. I'm trying to help her out." He turned back to Sophia. "Richie won't be meeting you. You understand? He's gone."

"No."

"Get off here. If you've got some money, you can get anywhere pretty fast."

"I'll get off with you," Susan said.

A few of her friends tried to dissuade her.

"We really can't be debating this for too long."

The two young women got off the bus. Everyone else was furious with Steve. Maybe they should've gotten off too, but they didn't. They seemed to have a lot of confidence in the fact that they were American girls on an American highway.

Steve spotted the escort car about 40 miles from Los Angeles. It was a little black Acura with tinted windows. They stayed in front of Steve the whole time. He followed them right to USC. The girls squawked a lot about this when Steve told them to get off. It wasn't the first time an entire busload of people had despised him, but it was the first time he'd ever gotten this much hate for trying to save someone's life.

It wasn't until he got them moving off the bus that he realized he was probably risking his own skin. It was also the first time he thought about how much money might have been in Sophia's little backpack. He remembered the way she'd said—*I have money*. He should've grabbed her bag at that gas station and run. Left the girls with all the problems, his bus and his failing business. But if he'd done that, he could just imagine the result: sixteen healthy young women chasing him across a traffic median.

Steve followed the last girl off the bus. It looked like there were spotters on either side. He got back in and drove away from campus. The drop was a 40-minute drive. The same man as before called.

"She better be on that bus," he said.

"She is. Lying down in the back."

Had he really just given up his life for the snotty girlfriend of some bigshot crook? He regretted it now. He'd always liked to think that he didn't really care whether he lived or died. But now that death looked like a real possibility, he didn't want it. Not without a fight. But what could he do?

Ernesto answered on the first ring.

"Hey, I've got a little trouble here," Steve said.

"I'm sure you'll figure it out."

"Do you care what happens to this girl?"

36

"No. But I care about you, man. That's the only reason I picked up the phone. Those guys won't hurt you if you cooperate. Just be sensible."

It probably was true that the advice came out of friendship, but it was also true that Ernesto had set him up in the first place. Send her to the states to get whacked. If they wanted the girl dead, weren't there much easier ways to do it back home?

"Next time you come down, we'll have seafood, you'll get the rest of your money, maybe I'll have something else for you to take back up."

"Good bye, Ernesto."

He could stop the bus and run for it. Leave it behind. The guys in the Acura would probably go for the bus first. It would take them more than a few seconds to figure out the girl wasn't on board. And Steve had 4500 dollars on him. Enough to get to Vegas. He could reinvent himself as a canny gambler, suave roller of dice.

There was another option. He could sell out the girl. He could find out where they were then tell the boys in the Acura that Sophia had figured out something was up, pulled a gun on him and made him stop the bus. She got off maybe 30 miles into America. But Steve could help them find her.

There were a lot of problems with that story, but if he could lead them to the girl, what reason would they have to kill him? He called Susan.

"Hey, this is Steve the bus driver. Can you put Sophia on the phone?"

Sophia came right on, impatiently.

"Yes?"

"I just heard from Richie. I don't know how he got my number, but he can come pick you up. Where are you right now?"

"He's not hurt? Richie is not hurt?"

"He sounded okay. He wants to pick you up. Are you still around where I left you? Have you moved?"

Dan heard a sound, a little hum, a lower voice than Sophia's. Then ten seconds of silence. Dan could picture Susan shaking her head at Sophia.

"I can't talk now," Sophia said and hung up.

Dan called back. Voicemail. He called back three more times. They weren't going to answer. A smart California girl had just signed his death warrant. Smart but vulnerable. It might not save his life, but he had one more play here. He sent a text: "I can say Sophia is traveling with Susan Lim, chemical engineer from Caltech. You'll have a pretty difficult semester."

Less than two hours ago, he'd been acting on the noblest impulses—selflessly saving children. Now he was threatening college girls with death to save his own sorry ass. A text came back a minute later: fuck you, partybus2000. When he came to a red on Hoover, he opened the door and took off running. Steve had gotten older since the last time he'd had to make a real dash for anything. He was slow and jiggly.

Maybe most of the guys went for the bus, but one of them chased Steve. There was too much open ground. He wasn't going to lose this younger, faster man, so he ducked into a donut shop. The man stayed outside at first, but when Steve got a Boston cream and a cup of coffee, the man came in.

"You know, you left your party bus back there," he said.

Steve shrugged and the man read something off his phone.

"So where is she?"

Steve shrugged again.

"I'll shoot you right here. Then I'll walk out the door. We'll find her another way. Or you come with me, take a ride, and we can figure things out like intelligent people."

Steve shook his head.

"I'm going to count to three."

Steve took another bite of donut and smiled.

The
SWEETHEART
SOUR
A Cheap Thrill
By: J.D.
GRAVES
PROMOTES
LITERACY

CHET-SHAPED LURE
Serena Jayne

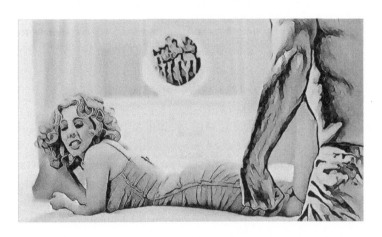

When GEEKGRL18 bit at his Chet-shaped lure, Darren could hardly contain his joy. His plan to borrow his brother's awesome Chet-ness to reel in one hot honey was nothing short of epic.

Sick to death of always coming up short in comparison to his older brother, Darren had logged into Chet's online dating profile and went fishing for ladies. Darren never stood a chance of bagging the top-notch babes his brother attracted. A bait and switch tactic was his best hope.

Chet's tall frame, chiseled abs, and razor-sharp cheekbones scored him work as a menswear model. His genius intellect earned him a full ride at Northwestern, where he enrolled in their pre-med program. His charisma won over both sexes, ensuring he never needed to pay a speeding ticket and scoring him plenty of free drinks.

Shorter by six inches, with the metabolism of a bear in hibernation, and a low C average at the local community college, Darren couldn't charm his way out of a fifty-cent late library book fine. The only free drinks Darren received were cups of tap water. He was at best the fun house mirror reflection of Chet.

The woman, who Darren had wooed for weeks with cyber winks and private messages sent from his brother's online dating account, had arrived at Lush Lounge late, clad in an all-black ensemble. She wore her hair tucked under a Cubs baseball cap.

Chet, a diehard Sox fan, would've hated the hat, but Darren never gave a crap about Chicago teams. Always getting chosen last in gym class had soured him on sports.

Her profile picture, a grainy and dark image, didn't do the real woman justice. She wasn't a perfect ten in the looks department, but she was a solid four points higher on the beauty scale than any woman Darren had dated. A point higher in the flesh than the eight he'd scored the photo she'd posted. Only her sensuous curves and full pink lips hinted at softness. Her cheekbones and pointy chin appeared sharp enough to slice.

Without making a single comment on the dissimilarity between Darren in the flesh and Chet's dating site photo, she focused her intense gaze upon him.

His dick went rock hard. As his blood rushed downward, he mentally reached for a Chet-ism for guidance:

to make a woman your bitch, become an alpha dog.

"White wine," he shouted to the bartender and scooted his bar stool closer to hers.

She shook her head and angled her body away. "Corona."

"Figured a classy chick like you would be a wino."

Her nose wrinkled as though he'd accused her of being a hirsute hobo guzzling swill from a brown-bagged bottle.

"A wine drinker, I mean," he said. "A genuine connoisseur, who does the whole sniff, swirl, and spit routine."

"You figured wrong." She broke eye contact and tapped on her cell phone until the barkeep returned with her beverage.

Darren grabbed the beer bottle from the bar, ready to squeeze the lime protruding from the neck.

Her eyes narrowed and her mouth twisted into the expression his third grade teacher, Mrs. Slaughter, wore whenever he'd peed his pants. The look that shriveled his insides and hurt his heart.

With the tip of her finger, she stabbed the citrus slice into the beer. The liquid foamed. She tilted the bottle and took a sip.

He ran his shaky hand through his thinning brown hair and pretended to watch the Blackhawks game on the big screen television. A defenseman blocked a shot on goal and the crowd cheered.

Darren's awkward antics had earned him plenty of quality time in Mrs. Slaughter's naughty corner. If he couldn't edge his way out of GEEKGRL18's penalty box, soon it would be game over for him. He'd invested too much time and energy in luring her to give up without scoring even a kiss. And he wanted more than a nibble.

He wanted the whole damned fish taco.

Instead of simply trying to act like his brother, he needed to somehow become him.

He cleared his throat and stuck out his hand. "I'm Chet."

"No. Tonight, you're Gary."

Her words hit him with the force of a knee to the kidney. He was out of his league, losing all control of the situation and any chance of getting laid. Without borrowing his brother's innate Chet-ness, he was doomed to be dumped before they even left the bar.

"Gary is an old dude's name." His voice went all kinds of whiney. "Please, call me Chet."

She stood and pushed in her stool.

His arms jerked the same way they did the last time Chet took him out on Lake Michigan and a muskie broke Darren's line. No way was he letting this fish get away.

"Please don't leave. I'm cool with role playing. Gary it is." His brother tended to date girls whose name ended with an I. "Can I call you Kati?"

"No. My game. My rules. No negotiation."

At his nod, she settled back onto her stool.

He reached into his shirt to rub the silver-plated charm on his necklace for luck. The bimbo at the jewelry store had raised her eyebrows at his request for the WWCD engraving, but having the mantra near his heart renewed his faith in the possibility of transforming into some semblance of his big brother, and in the process tapping into his awesomeness.

"What should I call you then? GEEKGRL18?" He let out a little laugh, imagining screaming out her user name while being balls deep inside her.

"For this game, all that matters is *your* name."

Like always, Darren had a Chet-ism handy. Do whatcha gotta do to get laid. Don't sweat the details.

GEEKGRL18 wasn't one for casual conversation. She finished her beer in silence, unresponsive to Darren's attempts to break the awkward tension. When she'd suggested they head to her place for a night cap, his shoulders finally relaxed. He'd had no idea how exhausting figuratively stepping into Chet's size thirteen loafers could be.

Luckily, she volunteered to drive. He avoided the whole explanation of why he didn't own a car, which inevitably led to him making excuses for living with his parents.

She tuned the car's sound system to a channel playing classic rock and drove. For the first fifteen minutes, Darren pondered his strategy. With a hairband singer crooning out a love ballad, he took the opportunity to employ another Chet-ism: *to conquer a woman, stake your claim on her territory* and placed his hand on her thigh.

She jerked the steering wheel and the sedan tore a diagonal path across the expressway. Tires squealed and car horns blasted around them. Her ball cap slipped off and her wild curls slithered to her shoulders.

It wasn't until they'd arrived at their destination and she'd parked that he'd stopped hyperventilating. He followed her into an old house in the outskirts of Elgin.

Every accessory in her home, from the carefully arranged fashion magazines on the coffee table to the framed abstract art, reminded him of the bland unlived-in perfection of a furniture showroom. Except for the bedroom.

He nearly gagged on the cloying stink of cheap aftershave. The strength of the odor made Darren wonder if

GEEKGRL18 watered the carpet with the vile stuff in an attempt to grow a garden of musky memories.

Hundreds of surveillance-style photos of a dark-haired dude covered the bedroom walls. So what if the faces of the people who appeared in the snapshots with the guy were crudely chopped out. Darren had torn up, torched, and otherwise mutilated his fair share of pictures of women who had rejected him.

Nothing about the man in the photos screamed special. The dude could play a dentist in a made-for-TV movie. In short, he had none of Chet's magic.

"That Gary?" He sat on the edge of the bed and slid off his sneakers.

"*You're* Gary tonight." She removed a pair of handcuffs, a length of rope, and a gag from a side table drawer. "Hush now."

The few women he'd dated weren't into props or anything exotic. They preferred any down and dirty action take place with the lights off. He couldn't wait to find out what he'd been missing.

One of his favorite Chet-isms was *kinky bitches are up for anything*. Darren held his wrists and feet still, allowing GEEKGRL18 to secure him to the wooden bed frame and to slip the gag into his mouth. Once she finished playing at being a dominatrix, she'd be obligated to turn his freaky fantasies into reality.

He'd go along with her games, but he'd never truly drop his Chet persona and don that of generic Gary. She could call him whatever she wanted, pretend he was someone else while touching him, because he'd be thinking of Chet, or rather of becoming his brilliant brother.

"Be right back, Gary." She ran her finger over one of the photos on the wall. "I'm going to slip into something more comfortable."

Darren enjoyed the view of her tight ass as she sauntered out of the room. While she was gone, he recited Chet-isms in his mind. What started as a way to pick up chicks had become his religion. He worshipped at the church of Chet.

She returned and he almost choked on his own saliva. Her "more comfortable" outfit was less suited for sex and more operating room or autopsy appropriate. She wore latex gloves and baby blue surgical scrubs—and brandished a mini blowtorch. The kind cooks used to toast the top layer of a crème brulee.

His body went cold and still, as though he'd swapped places with a dissection frog from high school science class.

If she'd themed her clothing to match the mini blowtorch in her hand by wearing the garb of a chef or welder, he might be able to laugh off her choice of attire. The maniacal glint in her eyes left no doubt that he was the only thing she intended on crisping.

"Until I met you, I never had the desire to pull the wings off butterflies or sizzle ants with a magnifying glass." Her voice with its acidic tone was barely audible over the whoosh of his rising blood pressure echoing in his ears. "You reshaped me into the woman I am today, Gary."

His heart pounded along with the phrase "what would Chet do" looping in his head. The WWCD mantra had gotten him into the situation and might be the only thing to get him out. He ran through his repertoire of Chet-isms, desperate to discover the words of wisdom to save his sorry skin.

The only thing Darren had going for him was his ability

to blend into the shadows while the spotlight illuminated his brother. His superpower stood little chance of being his salvation, because Darren had aimed the bright light upon himself. He lay pinned to the specimen tray of the bed, unable to channel his inner cockroach and scurry away.

She ignited the mini torch and stepped forward. "When you strung me along while looking for someone better, it burned. Now it's your turn to feel the heat."

Darren whimpered and fought his bindings. The bedframe shook, but his restraints held.

"NOT GARY," he screamed, the gag muffling his cry. "NOT GARY!"

She ran the edge of the flame along his arm in a scorching caress.

White hot pain blazed its way to his soul. He thrashed and gagged on the odor of burning hair and flesh.

"Don't worry, Gary. I haven't forgotten that ruggedly handsome face of yours."

He squeezed his eyes shut and tried to move away from the flame, but he was powerless to stop the agony. By the time she turned her attention to the other side of his face, everything mercifully went black.

Darren awoke with a whimper.

GEEKGRL18 stood over him holding his necklace in one hand and a cheese grater in the other. "WWCD? That some slut's initials?"

Darren tried to shake his head, but even the slightest movement cranked his pain level up to nuclear.

"If I could get away scot-free, I'd fillet your new girlfriend." She tossed the necklace, which landed on the edge of the mattress, and pressed the sharp side of the cheese grater against the ruined flesh of his cheek. "You're gonna love the santoku knife I picked up last week. I miss the goodies you used to cook for me. The way to my heart must have been through my stomach. We'll see if we can find a more direct route to yours."

He kept his gaze pinned to his WWCD charm and held his breath as she moved the grater through oozing flesh to bone.

Over the endless hours of suffering, Darren discovered that GEEKGRL18 possessed a seemingly endless supply of kitchen accessories and sought ways to used them that the manufacturers had never intended.

"Our game's getting boring." GEEKGRL18 made an exaggerated yawn.

Not wanting to see the instrument of torture du jour, Darren kept his attention focused on the WWCD charm. Even breathing hurt.

"You barely resemble a human being anymore, let alone a looker like Gary."

Darren couldn't wrap his mind around the idea of someone so beautiful being a monster inside. Of dying for the sins of some average Joe. If only he could teleport out of the torture chamber before she destroyed all that was left of him in her crusade to obliterate Gary.

"Lucky for me, there's an endless supply of Gary proxies on the internet," she said.

Tears rolled down his face, the salt making his damaged skin sting. Thanks to his never-ending faith in Chet's philosophies, she would release him and some other dude would take his place as her personal Gary voodoo doll.

His gaze pingponged between her venomous smile and

the shiny object in her hand.

"Gary always enjoyed tenderizing chicken breasts. That man was a god in the kitchen." She stepped forward, metal mallet raised. Her knee tapped the side of the bed and the necklace with the WWCD charm slithered out of sight.

Every ounce of hope that he could escape her scorching hatred of Gary turned to ash.

Chet would never be someone's sorry substitute. Darren might not be a player on the level of his brother, but he refused to meet his end as a garden-variety guy like Gary. So what if Darren was a mere cockroach compared to Chet's alpha dog.

With his lips clenched around his gag, he narrowed his eyes at GEEKGRL18. Cockroaches were survivors. No matter how much poison a person sprayed, the creepy crawlers always managed to scuttle away. Come hell or high water or nuclear war, those little bastards were here to stay. And so was he.

A new mantra started in his mind: *DARREN* on an endless loop. Screw that crazy bitch. He was one hundred percent Darren evermore.

When she raised the mallet, he didn't flinch, rather he fought his bindings with every ounce of Darren-ness in his being. Every not-so-perfect part of him came together in a manic melody of survival.

The headboard responded with a thunderous crack.

One hand free, he swung a bloody fist at GEEKGRL18.

Missed his target.

She stumbled backward, the mallet clutched to her chest. "Why couldn't you play your role? That's all I asked of you. But, no. You have to make things difficult, just the way the real Gary did. He'd screw with my emotions by sending mixed signals. Treat me like a booty call one minute and accuse me of being a psychopath the next."

Wiping away tears and snot with his elbow, Darren slid the gag down. "I would have done anything for you. Been anyone you wanted me to be. All I wanted was a chance to hook up with a girl like you. I'm nothing like that Gary jerk and you hurt me. Hurt me bad." He rattled the headboard. "You were going to k-k-kill me."

"Is it true you'd do anything for me?" She cocked her head. "Or is that a filthy lie, Chad?"

"I'm not Gary. Not Chad. Not Chet." He squared his shoulders. "I'm Darren."

"Darren." On her lips, his name was downright delicious. "I like the idea of having a special someone in my life who is devoted to my every need. That kind of a guy would be a keeper. Not someone I'd beat to death, dismember, and then throw away." GEEKGRL18 carefully laid the mallet on the floor and crept closer, palms outstretched. "No need to glare at me. I already told you that I no longer see you as Gary. You'd make a great caretaker for the next Gary and all those that follow. I promise to play your nursemaid until you're healed. What do you say? Partners?"

Darren had never been anyone's partner outside of his assigned middle school field trip buddy. Never been anything more than a glassy-eyed devotee of his brother. Never been more than a sad stalker of women. He liked the idea of being a part of a duo. Even a screwed up, codependent, murderous relationship beat the grim alternative of dying alone.

GEEKGRL18 must see something inside Darren, some

lost part of herself that made them soulmates, too de-
mented and too damaged for anyone but each other. Together they could conquer a world of Gary substitutes.
And maybe, just maybe, if he was a good little minion,
she'd reward him by spreading those long, luscious legs
and letting him have his wicked way with her. He'd bag
a grade-A babe with his endless enthusiasm and diehard
dedication.

"Well?" She shook the mallet.

Darren shrugged. "Why the hell not?"

Chet would never consider such a ludicrous proposal.
But Darren's desire to hear GEEKGRL18 scream his
name, either in passion or pain, was worth the risk of a
double cross.

He took a deep breath and created his first Darren-
ism: *psycho chicks need love too.*

HELL
CHOSE
ME

ANGEL LUIS COLÓN

THE GOON SQUAD
John Kojak

A psychiatrist once told me I lacked empathy. I told him that was bullshit—I just don't care. People die everyday. In the end it really doesn't matter how they died, or that they died at all. Not to me. My name is Mike Ellis. I'm a retired Army Master Sargent who survived two tours in Iraq and a stint with Special-Ops in Afghanistan. After I left the Army, I joined an elite team of men. Good men. Patriots. Our official designation was Presidential Task Force 45, but we called ourselves The Goon Squad. Our mission was to track down and kill people who, technically at least, had not yet committed a crime. But they would…deadly crimes.

How did we know? The way I heard it, an old bowlegged black janitor named Charlie Sumlin found one of those institutional green government-issue notebooks when he was cleaning out an old 1920's era Marine Corps barracks buildings on the grounds of the FBI headquarters in Quantico. He said the notebook was sitting alone on a shelf inside a closet that had been sealed off for decades behind dozens of rows of boxes stacked floor to ceiling. There was nothing on the outside, except the word NOTEBOOK printed in bold black letters on the front. But inside, there was a hand-written list of names, dates, and descriptions of horrible crimes:

Theodore I. Divine 11/06/14
Mass Shooting, Chuck E Cheese Kissimmee, FL
32 Dead

Caleb P. Hancock 09/05/15
Sniper Attacks, Capital Hill Washington, D.C.
9 Dead

Hassan A. Youssef 12/25/17
Car Bomb, Freedom Tower New York, NY
26 Dead

Raymond H. Cain 05/15/18
Arson, Eos Building Palo Alto, CA
67 Dead

The notebook was full of them.

Charlie recognized the first name on the list. Teddy Divine, the nineteen-year-old malcontent who had walked into a crowded Chuck E. Cheese in Florida with an AR-15 assault rifle and slaughtered seven adults and twenty-five children. But he said it was the second entry that really surprised him. On September 5th 2015, the day before he found the notebook, Jebediah Jackson, the Senior Senator from Tennessee, had been shot and killed on the steps of the Capitol Building. He was the first politician to be assassinated in Washington since President Garfield was shot in the back at a D.C. train station in 1881.

There were several other shootings around the capital the next day, a policeman was shot near the Treasury Building in the morning, a Saudi diplomat was killed as he walked out of the Kuwaiti Embassy around noon, and a retired IRS agent took a bullet in the head that evening while he was pumping gas at a Shell station, two blocks from the Lincoln Memorial. The news channels began calling the shooter The Capital Hill Killer.

Charlie looked back down at the notebook. Caleb P. Hancock09/05/15Sniper AttacksCapital HillWashington, D.C. 9 Dead He couldn't believe it. Neither could the FBI agents he showed the notebook to later that night. They thought the old guy had a few brooms missing from his closet—until they checked The National Crime Center Database. A former Marine sniper named Caleb Hancock was wanted in Tennessee in connection with his wife's murder. Her body had been found inside the couple's trailer outside of Nashville three days before Senator Jackson was shot. She died from a single gunshot wound to the chest from a high caliber 7.62mm bullet. The same type of round used in the Marine Corp's Remington M24 sniper rifles, and the same type of bullet that killed the Senator.

The Capital Police put the entire D.C. area in lockdown, and the FBI launched a nationwide manhunt for Hancock, but he was still able to kill five more people before they caught him at a police checkpoint near the 14th Street Bridge.

After Hancock was arrested, the notebook, and the strange story behind its discovery, was taken to the FBI Director. When they found the next name on the list, Hassan Youssef, working as a security guard at the Freedom Tower garage under a false identity three days later the notebook went all the way up to President William Stroker, the 45th President of the United States. He ordered the formation of Task Force 45 the next day.

He never served, but Old Willie liked to portray himself as a modern day Audie Murphy when it came to fighting terrorism. He made it clear that no quarter would be given to the people on the list. Age, gender, family status, nothing would matter. Everyone in the notebook was to be systematically eliminated in the order their names appeared on the list. Period.

Five men were selected for Task Force 45. Henry Wallace and I were former Army Special-Ops. Henry was tall and skinny, and parted his chestnut brown hair neatly to the side. He looked like the kind of guy you would meet at one of your kid's soccer games, but he was the most lethal man I ever met. Joe Jessup and Kevin Stone were FBI. They looked exactly like you would expect them to look, tall and meaty with short-cropped hair, cheap suits, and rubber soled leather shoes. They didn't talk much, but they followed orders—no questions asked. The last member of the Goon Squad was named Carlos Zepeda. He was a short bull of a man with intense brown eyes, bronze colored skin, and a thick black mustache that would've made a seventies porn star jealous. He was DEA. That's all I knew about him. That, and you didn't want to cross him. Five men who all had one thing in common—we were killers. Not murderers, per se, but men who would do anything to protect our country.

My first assignment was a skinny, horse-faced kid named Raymond Cain. Raymond was a twenty-two-year-old computer science major at Stanford University who looked like he was going to trip over himself every time he moved. I followed Raymond around for a week looking for clues, anything that would reveal how a nerdy guy like him would go from the Deans List to the hit list, but he never did anything remotely out of the ordinary. If there was a sinister side to him, I couldn't see it. But the notebook said he was going to burn down a building and kill sixty-seven people—so I put a bullet in his head.

Raymond wasn't my first kill. I put a lot of bodies in the ground in Iraq and Afghanistan, but that was war, this was different. I won't lie; in the split second before I pulled the trigger, a flash of doubt ran through my mind like a speeding train. *Maybe Charlie was full of shit?* But it wasn't my call. If your name was in the notebook, you were as good as dead. And that's the way it was. One kill after the next, we worked our way down the list with brutal efficiency. I never asked any questions, and I never had any regrets. That is, not until my last assignment—the Sutton's.

John and Anna Sutton were a young married couple in Texas. We usually worked alone, but the powers that be thought Henry and I should do this one together. I didn't have a problem with that, or the fact I got assigned the woman.

John was a lineman with the local telephone company.

He was tall and lean, with the understated muscularity of a man who works outside. His wife Anna was short and petite, and didn't look like she could bend a flower. The only thing that really stood out to me about her was her hair. It was black as a Kentucky coal and fell in waves down her back. It was the same type of hair I had seen in Iraq. The women over there would hide their hair under a head scarf, or hijab, in public, but once inside their homes they would take them off and the most luxurious dark silky hair would come tumbling out...those women were as beautiful as they were dangerous.

Henry followed John, and I watched Anna. John left home early and didn't usually get home until after dark. Anna didn't work, and never left the house before noon. Their routines were pretty consistent, until the day that Anna went to see a doctor, an OBGYN. I wasn't expecting that. She didn't look pregnant—but she never wore tight cloths either. I broke protocol later that day and followed her inside a Whole Foods Market. I might not look like it, but I know a thing or two about pregnant women. I walked up next to her in the seafood department and asked her if she knew if it was okay for a pregnant woman to eat shellfish. It was like ringing a bell, and once she got going she wouldn't stop talking about all the foods her doctor said pregnant women shouldn't eat. The longer she talked, the worse I felt about what I had to do.

That evening I called our commander, Colonel Bill Shine. He was a good man, and I figured that if anyone could talk the president into allowing us to bump the Sutton's down the list, he could. Hell, according to the notebook at least, it would be seven more years before John and Anna would blow themselves up in the middle of a crowded New Years Eve party. I didn't know why, the notebook never told you why. But whatever their reasons, the kid was surely innocent. That didn't matter to President Stroker though. He was adamant, no exceptions.

I didn't like it, but we had our orders, and as Henry and I formulated our plan we never mentioned it again. Anna Sutton was a target, just like her husband; there was no need to make things complicated.

The Sutton's lived in a little one-story brick home in a quiet rural area north of Houston. The house sat on a large lot, with a thick strand of tall pines in the front and back. There were no neighbors for a hundred yards on each side. It was perfect. We made sure there were no dogs, or alarms we needed to worry about, and then approached the house from the rear one night around three o'clock in the morning. Henry was good with locks, he was good at a lot of things besides just killing, and we slipped in through the back door without making a sound.

Not that it would have mattered. No one in that house would have heard a damn thing. John was sleeping on his back with his mouth open snoring like a pig that swallowed a rattlesnake. Anna was lying in bed next to him, curled up in the fetal position with one arm cradling the small bump in her belly, and the other clutching a pillow tightly over her head. I wondered how many nights she had lied there wishing that something, anything, would shut him up. The irony was too dark, even for me.

Henry took the right side of the bed, next to John, and I took the left. We raised our silenced .22 caliber pistols and fired two shots each. Anna's arm slid slowly off of the pillow, and when it tumbled to the floor I could see her face in the moonlight. Her thick black hair helped cover the entrance wound, and she looked like she was sleeping peacefully. I was thankful for that. I glanced over at John. He had the same stupid slack-jawed look on his face; the only difference now was the silence. Henry and I left the way we had come in, and drove off in separate cars without saying a word.

I never saw Henry after that. And I never got another assignment. A few months later Willie Stroker lost his re-election bid to a young senator from Massachusetts. Task Force 45 was officially disbanded the next day.

I didn't mind too much. I was finally able to stop killing and start living. I moved to Jacksonville and bought a boat, a forty-three foot cabin cruiser with twin 484hp diesels and upgrades out the wazoo, and started a charter fishing business. Every morning I would take car salesman, stockbrokers, and tourist out looking for marlin, kingfish, or whatever else was biting. Most of the time my clients didn't even care if they caught anything, they just wanted to get away from their wives and get drunk for the day. It was a good life. And, over time, the wars, and the faces of those I killed, began to fade.

But karma's a bitch that never forgets. A few years later I took a group of rich bankers out trolling for swordfish. One of them ended up hooking an eight-foot tiger shark instead. He didn't mind, they might not be good eating, but tigers always put up a hell of a fight. Once we got the shark onboard, I did what I always did. I bled and gutted it. A lot of the usual junk came tumbling out: a half-eaten Mahi-Mahi, a baby squid, a couple of empty beer cans, a dolls head, and a plastic water bottle. I was about to sweep it all over the side when I noticed a small piece of paper rolled up inside the plastic bottle. I didn't think much about it at first; a message in a bottle makes about as much sense as a letter to Santa Claus. But for some reason, maybe it was the half-faded memories of the note-book, I picked up the bottle, twisted off the cap, and used my deck knife to reach in and pull out the thin roll of paper. When I unrolled it, I saw that it contained a list of names.

Henry Wallace
Joe Jessup
Kevin Stone
Carlos Zepeda
Mike Ellis

A cold shiver shot up my spine.

I high tailed it back to port and made a few phone calls. The first was to Henry Wallace's wife. She told me they had been eating Chinese take-out one night, about a year ago, when Henry opened a fortune cookie and turned white as a ghost. He wouldn't tell her what it said, and when she got up in the morning he was gone. Two months later she got a call, the police found Henry face down in a duck pond with two bullets in the back of his head. Next I called Bill Shine. He hadn't heard about Henry, but told me that Joe Jessup and Kevin Stone had died in a single car accident on a small deserted road in Iowa. No one knew for sure, but the local cops said it looked like they were running from something. It took awhile, but when I finally tracked down Carlos Zepeda, I learned he had been found tied to a fence post outside Tucson wearing a Columbian necktie.

Somehow, no one put it all together. And I didn't tell them about the note I found inside the shark either. It wasn't so much that I didn't expect them to believe me, but sometimes things are coming and there's no way to stop them. I think the other guys knew that too.

I can't tell you how it happened. One morning my boat might have blew up, or maybe a shooter posing as a middle-school teacher put a couple of bullets in the back of my head and dumped me overboard. In the end, I guess it doesn't really matter how it happened, or that I died at all. But if you're reading this, the last of the goons is gone.

THE NIGHT AND THE LAND

MATT SPENCER

THE NIGHT JAKE ADDSION SAVED THE WORLD
Donald Jacob Uitvlugt

Jake Addison sensed the lights before he saw them. He felt that little prickle along the back of his neck that had saved him many times before. He froze, willing the shadows of the trees around the clearing to cover him. Then the lights appeared.

Not headlights. He was too far into the woods even for a truck shining for deer. The lights shone through the trees, three of them, pale green. They circled for a moment, spinning around each other and around Addison's head. Then they shot off in the direction of town.

Addison frowned. It was a sign. Of what, he did not yet know, but nothing happened by chance. Jeremiah twenty-nine eleven He took up his shovel again and began filling up the hole he had made. He wondered if the woman had seen the lights and what she thought of them. She moaned softly through her gag as shovel-loads of dirt rained down on her face.

It was so much work, purifying this one corner of the Earth. Best to finish up tonight and worry about what the lights meant later.

Addison was still puzzling over the lights three days later as he sipped his coffee in Ida's Diner, reading the paper. Kendall County's *Weekly Herald*. The coffee was a weakness, and Ida's coffee was excruciatingly bad. If he was going to indulge in a vice, he was going to make darned sure he didn't enjoy it.

The paper was another matter. The paper was business. Addison found the police blotter. Still no mention of the young woman. That was good. Other notices had him puzzled, though.

Twice last week the police had been called out to homes near Unwin Woods. Strange lights and noises. Dogs barking up a storm, but not willing to go into the trees.

Addison saw there were fewer vagrancy arrests than usual. Very strange. There were always people wandering through town this time of year. Vacationers taking back roads to Lake Michigan. Migrant workers looking for employment on nearby farms. Drifters blown toward

Kendall County like dust collecting in a forgotten corner of the universe.

For there to be no reports on the flotsam and jetsam of society was suspicious. Besides the fact that a lack of vagrants was bad for Addison's vocation. Then there was the notice that George Miller was missing. The Miller's farm was not far from the dirt track Addison used to get into the woods. He'd spent many a pleasant afternoon chatting with the man, Addison in his truck, Miller sitting in a chair on his lawn.

Something was happening. He had plenty of work to do. The new moon was a few days away. But he did not like the feeling in the air.

"Freshen you up, Jake?"

"Yes. Thank you, Ida. Could you fill up a thermos for me too? It's going to be a long day."

In spite of his suspicions, Addison's preparations for the upcoming new moon went perfectly. He drove his battered Ford out to the Big Lake, watched the revelers on the beach trying to pretend late September was still summer. It had taken Addison until sunset to single out a victim.

Young, unblemished. Last year of high school or first year of college, if Addison were forced to guess. Jeans and t-shirt that had been faded by the manufacturer rather than hard work under the summer sun. A male this time, though that didn't matter much.

A group started a bonfire on the beach after the sun set. Addison's quarry did not join in but remained on the fringes, sitting on the bumper of a Corvette half-smeared with primer. Addison decided it was time.

"Not going to join the party?"

The youth jumped at the sound of Addison's voice. "No. Couldn't scam the booze. No booze, you're not welcome." He tried to sound calm, though Addison could all but hear his pulse race, all but smell the first sweat of fear.

Addison held up the six-pack he had carried from his truck. The aluminum cans clinked softly. "I'd be glad to share."

The youth eyed Addison up and down, calculating what price he would have to pay. Addison chuckled, a sound like the crinkling of fall leaves.

"I ain't queer, if that's what you're wondering. I just remember what it was like to be young and on the outside looking in."

Doubt and desire battled in the young man's eyes. Addison pulled one of the beers from its plastic noose.

"It's perfectly fine. See."

He popped the beer open and pretended to drink. The youth smiled at last, took the rest of the six-pack.

"Thanks, man. If there's anything I can ever do for you…"

He trailed off, covering his returning nerves by popping open a beer of his own and taking a swig. He started for the party. And then the drugs Addison had put in the beer kicked in.

"As a matter of fact, yes. There may be something you can help me with."

Addison put his arm around the youth before his legs crumpled from under him and half walked, half dragged him to the truck. If anyone from the bonfire saw, they would have thought he was one of their own, helping a friend who had had too much. Addison grunted as he lifted the youth into the cab of the Ford and covered him with an old blanket.

Addison hummed along with the oldies playing on the radio as he drove to his cabin on the edge of Unwin Woods. He rubbed the doorframe gently as he unlocked the door. Here was where he had received his calling, and that was still where he prepared his offerings. After carrying the young man into the small but tidy wood building, he stripped the young man of his clothes. No tattoos, no piercings or other bodily impurities. Leviticus one. Addison had chosen well. He wondered if the young man was a first-born son.

He tied him to the bed in his guest room and gagged him with a white cotton towel. It took three days to purify the young man's system. Addison bathed him every day with water from the spring out back. He shaved him, cleaned up his waste, gave him nothing but spring water to drink through the cloth gag, until his urine ran as clear as the water.

Through this all, the youth went through the stages Addison had seen so many times before. The blank look of disbelief. The curses and threats through the gag. The tearful pleas. The sullen silence. And then the moment when the body went slack and Addison knew the youth had accepted his role to help purify the world.

That night was the night of the new moon. The young man gave only a token protest as Addison untied him from the bed and bound his hands and feet together. After days without food, he was much easier to carry to the truck than from it. Addison drove deeper into Unwin Woods. At the turnoff, he passed the Miller farm. The police still hadn't found George Miller. Addison shook his head. It was a wicked, wicked world they lived in. So few decent folks left.

Addison parked the truck at the end of the dirt trail.

The youth blinked at the flashlight as Addison gathered his supplies. A soft grunt as Addison pulled him down onto the stretcher he had prepared, lashing him into place. Addison was huffing and puffing by the time they reached the clearing for tonight's ritual.

No rest for him though, no matter how old and tired he felt. He took his shovel and pick from the stretcher and began to dig. It was close to midnight before Addison finished. He paused a moment to mop his brow, then untied the youth from the stretcher and rolled him into the pit he had dug.

When his watch chimed midnight exactly, Addison took four six-inch steel spikes and hammered them through the young man's wrists and ankles, nailing him naked and spread-eagle to the bottom of the pit. He moaned reflexively to the pain, even though he was a willing sacrifice. After he secured the youth, Addison pulled a knife across the stomach to open up his entrails.

Addison gathered his tools and climbed out of the pit. He had just taken up the shovel to fill in the pit when the hairs on the back of his neck prickled. He looked behind him. The lights were back. They wove among the trees like a trio of oversized, drunk fireflies. But this time they did not dart away. They drew closer to Addison, until he could see they were lit globes on the underside of a craft of some sort. A black shape, only slightly less dark than the moonless midnight sky. Addison could barely make out the shape of a triangle with the corners rounded off.

As Addison stood there staring, an opening dilated open in the underside of the craft. A beam of light shot out, blinding Addison. There was an intense sound, more felt than heard, rattling Addison from within until he blacked out from the pain.

* * *

Addison awoke gradually, blinking his vision clear. A quick look around him revealed that he was naked, bound spread-eagle, not flat on his back but raised on an incline of perhaps thirty degrees. The irony of his position did not escape him, and he managed a half-smile. Then he took a look at his surroundings.

He was in a room about half the size of his cabin. The walls were a dark ashen grey. It looked like someone had taken stalactites and melted them together, or perhaps had woven together the intestines of a giant. There were protuberances irregularly spaced on the walls. They may have been control devices of some sort, or perhaps were just cancerous growths on the bowels of the craft. For Addison had no doubt he was inside the ship he had seen.

A being appeared without Addison seeing how he arrived. One moment he was alone in the room, the next there was a presence like a hum in his mind. Addison craned his head and saw a being in a roughly human shape with an elongated face and two huge black eyes. A slit for a nose, a longer slit for a mouth. Though it was perhaps only two-thirds of Addison's height, the elongated limbs and fingers gave it a spritish appearance.

It was either naked or wore a tight suit the same grey of its face. Addison saw no identifiable sexual characteristics at all.

And it was sick. His calling had made him sensitive to impurities, and Addison could feel the being's illness emanating from it in fetid waves. It turned to depress some of the wall tumors, and Addison saw a growth on its right side like lichen eating away at a rock or leprosy breaking down human flesh.

Addison fought against his urge to rage at the being. He was a priest not a victim, and he would not act like a victim. There was something he was meant to learn here. Something he was meant to do. He was used to biding his time until the moment was right. He would wait until that moment, act, and then return to his true calling.

The creature kept at its business as if Addison wasn't in the room. It studied a number of the protuberances closely, caressing some of them with its long, slender fingers, pressing others until they disappeared into the walls. At last it departed, the walls parting for it like a giant hernia. Before the wall closed completely, another figure came through it. Addison could instantly put a name to the figure, though it would be a mistake to say that he recognized it. George Miller. It had been the lost farmer. Addison's stomach roiled at the unclean thing now standing in front of him.

Whatever lichenous leprosy infested the alien had taken strong root in Miller's body. Grey scabs covered most of his left half, a milky pus leaking from the gaps between them. His hair had started to fall out. The left eye had a grey film over it, and now looked neither alien nor human. Miller's genitals had been eaten away by the infection, and he stank like the grave.

But the worst of it, the very worst, was that Addison could see the infection at work. It pulsed as it fed, an irregular rhythm not born of Earth. The scabs danced and writhed, a slow waltz of extraterrestrial maggots, breaking down the flesh of George Miller and putting some hideous, unclean thing in its place.

"Hello, Jake."

It was but wasn't Miller's voice. The articulation was off, as if the mechanism was breaking down. Or the

72

operator was not familiar with it.

"Hello, George. How you doing?"

A grim parody of a smile. "I've been better. You?"

"Except for an itch I can't scratch, I'm doing fine."

The Miller-thing thought this immensely funny, doubling over in a wheezing laugh like acid eating away at stone.

"You always did have a dry sense of humor, Jake. I bet you wonder what you're doing here."

"Nope. I think I've got it pretty well figured out."

The thing looked at him in disbelief, blinking its dead eyes. Addison went on.

"Whatever is flying this thing got kicked off its own world. Maybe it abused it until the planet vomited it out. Maybe they're just walking mold spores. Infect a planet, consume it like a rotting orange, move on to the next.

"Regardless, they found their way here. They're taking a little taste, seeing if life here agrees with them. If it does, they plan on staying. Spreading their putrescence over the planet."

As if we aren't doing a good enough job of ruining it ourselves, Addison thought. As if his priesthood wasn't hard enough before. Now this.

The Miller-thing frowned as it considered Addison's words. He had made it mad. Good. Angry people were stupid people.

"The Valutu are superior to us in every way, but they are dying. They need our help. They've chosen the human race because our DNA and brain chemistry are compatible with theirs. Once they've joined with us, they can teach us so much."

Addison snorted. "Rape from the stars is still rape. The Earth has been violated enough without you adding your filth." He studied the Miller-thing dispassionately. "Tell me, George. Did it hurt when they 'joined' with you? Did you scream? Or did you take it like a cheerleader behind the bleachers?"

Wham. Addison's head flew back at the force of the blow. Perhaps there was something of Miller left in the creature after all.

"I hear your wife has stopped looking for you, George. Such a sad situation for her. Good thing Ben de Witt is so willing to offer his comfort at a time like this. Ready, willing, and able."

The Miller-thing pulled his arm back for another blow. Addison watched in amazement as a network of veins showed grey under Miller's remaining skin. The tempo of the irregular rhythm pulsing under the scabs grew faster. The writhing of the putrescence consuming the body sped up as well. Interesting. The rate of the illness increased with the intensity of Miller's emotions. The Miller-thing collapsed in pain, howling so loud it hurt Addison's ears.

The walls ruptured in three places, three of the scabrous aliens rushing in. Two of them picked the Miller-thing up off the floor and dragged it away. The third leveled a cylindrical object at Addison. A weapon of some sort, he guessed. Addison was not frightened. He had these creatures pegged.

The alien pressed a wall tumor that released Addison. As he got to his feet over the protest of his knees, the alien waved the cylinder at him.

"No funny business. I get it."

The creature marched him through the wall into a corridor like a long grey colon. They came at last to a large open space. The heart of the craft, Addison understood at once. His clothes had been piled to one side here, his tools with them. He supposed that his abductors wanted to leave no evidence.

But he hardly had time to take in his belongings when his attention was pulled to the center of the chamber. A column twisted up to the ceiling like the trunk of a tree covered in an ivy of grey intestines. Some of these tentacle-like tubes hung loose from the central shaft. More than a few ended in pointed spines, each longer than a hypodermic needle and dripping a milky grey fluid.

The alien behind him directed Addison toward the center of the room. Two of the stinger-tentacles stabbed out, pierced Addison's body, injected their poison and pulled out. He bit his lower lip, only letting out a slight gasp at the pain. It would be as it would be. He would remain calm. Micah six eight. He would show himself worthy of his calling.

He could feel the alien infection inside him, feel the filth coursing in his veins. To the pure, all things are pure. Addison hoped he had guessed correctly. If he had not, it would prove his unworthiness, and he would deserve what he got.

The alien behind him waited. The tentacles of the heart tree curled like snakes tasting the air. Addison could sense their expectation shift into confusion. Something should be happening by now and it wasn't. Addison smiled. It was time to strike.

He pivoted to the right, quicker than his alien escort. He snatched up his shovel from his things, swung it around, drove the blade into the alien's abdomen. Its body was like a tough gelatin, and when Addison withdrew the blade, it was covered in a green substance like plant sap.

The creature crashed to the floor like a felled tree. It had not fired its weapon. Perhaps it had not had time.

Perhaps it had not wanted to injure the central column. The walls of the heart chamber parted and more aliens rushed in, directed by the flailing tentacles of the central column. As they attacked Addison, he laid one low with the butt of the shovel. Another he brought down with a whack across the neck. Green soon coated the shovel from handle to blade.

When a dozen of the aliens lay on the floor, Addison found himself alone with the heart tree. He circled the perimeter of the chamber, staying out of reach of the stingers, quartering the aliens on the floor with a few strokes of his shovel's blade. He then went through his belongings on the floor until he found his knife.

With knife and shovel in hand, he turned to face the central column. Not knowing if it understood him and not really caring, Addison began to speak.

"You thought you could pollute the Earth with your filth. You thought wrong. I am the chosen to renew the Earth. A pure and spotless offering renews her. But you, you will be cut down and burned."

The tentacles reared up and struck Addison again and again. The stings hurt, but they did not bring him down. With knife and shovel, Addison began to hack the tentacles off, one by one.

"Your other poor victims were easy prey. It's human passion, human emotions that spread your infection in their systems. The more scared or the angrier they got, the faster the infection grew in them."

The tentacles attempted to escape him now. They writhed away, but the strokes of Addison's knife were swift and sure.

"But I am the chosen of God. I know no fear. I have no anger. I am on the narrow path of righteousness. I am the purification of God."

Addison took his shovel with both hands, slammed the blade into the heart tree again and again and again, until he sliced through the column. Green fluid sprayed everywhere. Addison felt the floor shake under his feet, and then grow still.

He had triumphed, as the righteous must always triumph.

Without its heart, the ship crashed in the clearing of Addison's most recent offering. It took him time to go through each chamber of the craft. He could do nothing for the infected wretches he found save put them out of their misery. Perhaps there was a look of gratitude on George Miller's face as Addison drove the shovel into him, but that might have been wishful thinking on Addison's part.

When he was sure everything was dead inside the craft, he hacked his way out through the bowel-walls. He took a moment to cover his neglected sacrifice with earth, knowing God would understand the irregularity. Then a hike to his truck to collect the gas can from the cab. Only one thing could purify this sort of uncleanness from the Earth. Fire.

The flames rose high as the new day dawned in Unwin Woods. He was going to lose so much time because of the aliens' interference. Seven days to see if he had contracted the infection after all. Leviticus thirteen. Seven days, and then a sacrifice of personal purification. When he was clean, he could again take up his mission to purify the Earth.

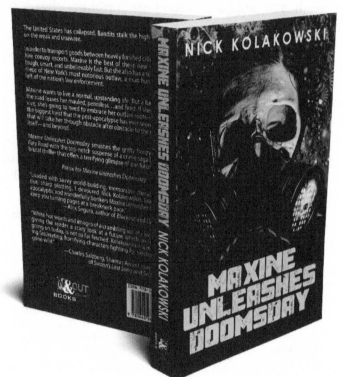

The United States has collapsed. Bandits stalk the high
on the weak and unaware.

In order to transport goods between heavily fortified citi
hire convoy escorts. Maxine is the best of these new
tough, smart, and unbelievably fast. But she also has a sc
niece of New York's most notorious outlaw, a man hun
left of the nation's law enforcement.

Maxine wants to live a normal, upstanding life. But a ba
the road leaves her mauled, penniless...and fired. If she
vive, she's going to need to embrace her outlaw roots—
the biggest heist that the post-apocalypse has ever seen
that will take her through obstacle after obstacle to the i
itself—and beyond

Maxine Unleashes Doomsday smashes the gritty, twisty
Fury Road with the top-notch suspense of a crime saga i
brutal thriller that offers a terrifying glimpse of our futur

Praise for *Maxine Unleashes Doomsday*

"Loaded with savvy world-building, memorable charac
cise, sharp plotting, I devoured Nick Kolakowski's *Ma*
apocalyptic and wonderfully bonkers *Maxine Unleashes* (
keep you turning pages at a breakneck pace."
—Alex Segura, author of *Blackout* and *De*

"White hot words and images of a crumbling soc...are lea
giving the reader a scary look at a future which, in li
going on today, is not so far fetched. Kolakowski's am
ing fascinating, horrifying characters fighting for exister
gone wild."
—Charles Salzberg, Shamus Award-win
of *Swann's Last Song* and *Se*

&OUT
BOOKS

ISBN 978-1-
9 781643 96

NICK KOLAKOWSKI

MAXINE UNLEASHES DOOMSDAY   NICK KOLAKOWSKI

MAXINE
UNLEASHES
DOOMSDAY

Pulp Modern

Tech Noir Special   Fall 2019

BREAKING BIZARRO

AN ANTHOLOGY

DEATH'S HEAD PRESS

SWITCHBLADE
Outlaw Fiction

ELEVEN ISSUES
PLUS TWO SPECIAL ISSUES

THE WORLD'S ONLY NO-LIMIT

NOIR DIGEST MAGAZINE

THE CURSE OF THE TEMPLE TOPAZ
Robb T. White

I had a sixth sense Donnie Milrath was going to be trouble on the job. He'd just completed a three-year bid for B & E at McAlester. A penitentiary you do not want to do time in, and he was jumpy, talking too fast on the ride back from LAX that morning when I met his flight from Oklahoma City.

Sean O'Reilly, on the other hand, was the same as our last job together three years ago in Belfast. An aging, international playboy, he looked like a cross between a baby-faced California surfer and a wrinkled Casanova who'd spent too many drunken nights in expensive brothels. We plucked three minor masterpieces off the walls of this rich collector's manor house in County Mayo.

But that was three years ago, and I'd long since blown that money at various Caribbean resorts.

The three of us were dining at the rescue mission off San Pedro. We had dozens of residents of L.A.'s Skid Row for dining companions, including a homeless man named Ralph from Boise who lived in a tent. He told me the goulash wasn't half-bad but "sometimes the bread is stale."

I'm keeping a low profile, while I scout the terrain for the upcoming job with Donnie and Sean. I could have had a safe 9-to-5 job with my degree in mining technology from the Colorado School of Mines. Color me the black sheep of my family.

I do what I do because I'm in love. The current object of my affection doesn't happen to be a woman but a chunk of rock. Topaz is a rainbow many colors, both light and dark shades; it can be as light as peach or pink to deep, vibrant reds, yellows, or a yellow-brown of Sherry. Blue is naturally rare but common on the market because of dyeing treatment. Golden topaz is the purest kind. Imperial topaz, like the famous Blaze in Chicago, is an eye-clean gemstone with few inclusions and a basal cleavage, meaning there's cleavage in only one direction parallel to the base. Some believe topaz has mythical properties, if you believe legends. Indians believe it unlocks the throat chakra.

Donnie insisted on staying at a motel rather than sleeping rough like me. Sean had no woman to crash with at the time so he pampered himself at a 4-star hotel near the airport.

At five-fifteen, Sean got out of a cab, smoothed trousers with a knife-sharp crease, and crossed the street at a trot when he spotted me.

"You didn't tell me this was a black-tie affair, Neill," he joked taking in my faded Metallica tee-shirt, dad Levi's, scuffed shoes, and Lakers ballcap.

"Just blending in," I replied. We shook hands. "Camouflage."

"Well done," Sean said. "You're definitely doing that. What kind of shithole part of town is this?"

"I assume your accommodations last night met your high standards?"

"Actually, no," Sean said. "Most unsatisfactory, actually. The pillows were definitely not goose-down as advertised and the speckled dace for breakfast was seriously underdone."

"Pity."

Two minutes later, I spotted a cab turning left from East Sixth onto San Pedro. Donnie emerged from the cab wearing sunglasses, which highlighted his prison pallor.

I introduced him to Sean.

"You English?"

Sean sniffed as if the word carried a transmittable disease. "Fortunately not, I'm Irish," Sean replied.

"Let's eat, gents," I interjected. "I'm starving."

Sean's gourmet sensibilities were offended by my choice of dining establishment, that men's shelter where volunteers served free food, but he's a professional. Donnie, on the other hand, could put the feedbag on with gusto whether in a prison chow line or a Chinese buffet.

Our first rendezvous was within walking distance of the target.

"Eat up," I said; "then we'll talk."

Sean pushed his paper plate aside and drew out a pack of cigarettes until a serving woman in an apron gave him a sharp look.

"Ha, she just mean-mugged you over that cigarette, O'Reilly. Reminds me of the joint," Donnie said. "Guy looks at you like that, he better be willing to go to war."

Sean ignored him.

"Neill, can we for the sake of sweet Jesus get down to business?"

"Try the pecan pie," I said, prolonging his distress for my own amusement.

He looked at it as if a tarantula had just walked over my plate.

Over coffee in Styrofoam cups, which Sean declined, calling it "liquid filth," I laid the plan out for them. All they knew prior to this was a vague reference to "contract work" I'd arranged out in L.A., which had to be done through third parties. Donnie knew even less than Sean. Gang intelligence staff study convict mail like scholars with a parchment from the Dead Sea Scrolls.

"Ever heard of the Bahia Emerald?"

Blank stares.

"It's known as the Curse of the Bahia Emerald," I said, and gave them a brief history of that massive emerald, as big as a dorm refrigerator and weighing as much as a couple NFL interior linemen.

"That huge-pound green rock," I said, "is worth hundreds of millions—or a hundred bucks, depending on which dealer you ask."

It had sucked in a bunch of dreamers, schemers, and losers into its orbit ever since a group of miners dug it out of the Brazilian soil, put it in a donkey cart and hauled it across the jungle and over a mountain.

85

"Right now," I said, "it's sitting in the L.A. County Sheriff's evidence locker a couple blocks from where we're sitting."

"You're shitting me," Donnie said. For the first time, he took his shades off and gave me a look into his eyes. I saw a junkie's eyes staring back at me.

"Lawyers are still fighting over who can claim it," I resumed. "They refuse to let anyone near it but they'll take photos of it lying in its rough wooden crate if you have a court order from one of the claimants. People have betrayed one another for it, some have died, and a few still wait around hoping luck will bless them and they'll get a stake in it."

"Neill, tell me you didn't make me get on a plane for this pipe dream," Sean said.

"Not the Bahia Emerald," I replied, laughing. "That thing is nothing, come right down to it, but a misbegotten mix of cylindrical emerald crystals sticking at odd angles from a mass of black schist."

"You mean because it's cursed?" Donnie asked.

Donnie, my boyhood amigo, won't be staying up nights worried about quark entanglement. He's muscle. He learned how to handle explosives on legit jobs in mining the same as me, only my specialty was never going to be drilling oil. I've known him since we were teens in the same juvie facility in Norman. I straightened out, got serious about my goals. Donnie followed another drummer. He did strongarm stuff after our gladiator school stint and wound up doing serious prison time. Our last job before this was a jewelry store in Boca Raton. I needed Donnie for one small task—set an explosion for a distraction and hightail it out of there. That was all. Sean O'Reilly might act like an ingénue who throws a temper over a cracked cuticle, but he's ex-IRA, very tough. I trusted both these guys.

"Relax," I said. "That thing's too big."

Donnie thought like a smash-and-grabber, one of those late-night thieves hauling an ATM machine out of a Dairy Mart chained to a stolen pickup. "Thing is, we'd never be able to sell it. It'd be like trying to sell the *Mona Lisa*."

"Then what exactly are we doing here in this fine establishment, Neill?"

I told them about the Temple Topaz.

"The...what?"

That, again, from Donnie.

"It's why you're here," I said and finished the dregs of my coffee. "It just happens to be locked up in the same facility with the Bahia Emerald."

Ever since I discovered the Temple Topaz was sitting in that warehouse with all kinds of evidence from L.A.'s violent past, I'd been unable to think of anything else. The twists and turns that got the Bahia Emerald inside that warehouse would take a book to explain, but the Temple Topaz winding up in there was a fluke, an afterthought. The Brazilian representative for the consortium of three American businessmen who bought it from the mine owner with the concession told them he could save them money if they didn't declare its value at Customs.

"Gentlemen," I concluded, "I have the exact place on the shelf where that rock is sitting. Tomorrow night we're going to get it."

They had questions—so many we had to leave just as the pamphlets with hymns were being handed round. We walked out into an early California evening. Foul odors wafted about. A homeless man pissed against a rusted fence across the street. Junk-food wrappers, empty plastic water bottles, and dog turds littered the sides of the road. My spirits soared as we walked to the car. Sean and Donnie peppered me with more questions.

"You're telling me we can just walk in there and walk out with it?"

"Yes, Sean, we can," I replied.

"How many guards?"

Donnie's question was accompanied by a hard grip on my bicep.

"Five," I said; "the warehouse is armed, CCTV cameras cover the grounds. The guards carry Sigs and Glocks."

"Aw, Neill," Sean complained, "this sounds like the OK Corral, not a gentlemanly heist."

"Look, the county doesn't have room for all the evidence they collect," I said. "They move the oldest evidence, all the cold and no-hope cases down to this warehouse. Their evidence depot on San Pedro got filled up. The topaz used to be kept behind a wire fence on a pallet along with the Bahia Emerald until the court ruled on it. Now it's kept inside a vault with no access, but the topaz is sitting in a box right inside that cement warehouse."

I pointed my finger in the direction we were walking.

"Rubbish, Neill, what the hell makes you think..."

"You're full of it, man," Donnie chimed in. "You dragged us out here for this? I just did time and I ain't so keen on going back inside."

I couldn't blame them. They didn't have my fever for stones. Until I heard about the Temple Topaz myself, I wouldn't have believed it.

I finally shut them both up by enunciating two words: *Six-teen mil-lion.*

Donnie and Sean halted at the same time; then, like a pair of *a capella* choirboys, they said at the same time: "What did you *saaaayy*?"

"You heard me," I replied. "Twelve million. Cash or bearer bonds, whichever you prefer. I've got the buyer lined up. Gilberto is meeting us in the Yucatan the week after next."

Donnie was speechless. For an Okie with a colorful vocabulary, that's saying something. Sean, on the other hand, looked serious, his forehead wrinkled. "You might have filled us in before this."

I said nothing but my reasons were obvious: Donnie was a jailbird and Sean was probably living off a woman somewhere.

"Let's get to the motel and work out the details. We're on a short timeline," I said.

I'd been reading the *L.A. Times*. The courts were going to rule on the claim to the Bahia Emerald. Somebody might wonder about the Temple Topaz and the error would be discovered, and all hope lost.

"How do you know they haven't moved the stone?" Donnie asked me on the way.

"I've got a guy on the inside," I said. "He's kept me informed."

"I love disgruntled employees," Sean said. "They make everything so much easier."

"This guy, Neill," Donnie asked me. "He think he's coming in for a cut?"

"He thinks I'm working for a rival claimant to the Temple Topaz. I told Sean I've been hired to keep tabs on it. I've been paying for his booze. He drives a tow-motor and makes three dollars above minimum."

"You're not worried he'll describe you down to your

hairy ginger eyebrows when that gemstone goes missing?"

"Not much," I replied. "He's got a ferocious drinking problem and he likes to bip at work."

"A vulgar Americanism, I assume."

"Dude snorts heroin and coke," Donnie told him.

Donnie rolled his eyes at me. He's been jugged more often for drugs than crime. He told me he made cash selling "candy blunts" to high-schoolers—blunts dipped in cough syrup.

I'd blown nearly all my money setting up this heist, and even though I'd done more complicated heists without an inside man, that twinge in my guts returned. What exactly it was, I couldn't have said. Twenty-four hours later, I had my answer.

By then it was too late. Way too late.

I'd never been mickey-finned before. It isn't like the movies. You don't wake up hollering, "I'll kill you, you dirty bastards!"

The nausea was excruciating. I vomited every few minutes while I stumbled around the room packing up. I recall heaving until my stomach settled again. Here I was, alone, betrayed, in a seedy Los Angeles motel, my wallet emptied, hugging the porcelain throne "calling the Irishman," as we used to say when one of us had too much to drink—you know, bellowing *O'Rourke* as we tossed our cookies. I was mentally invoking another Irishman while I heaved what was left in my stomach of the sour beer: *O'Reilly, I'll find you wherever you go...*

Donnie Milrath's betrayal stung worse; we were friends, crimeys together before we went our separate ways. Donnie must have been talked into it by Sean, the more cunning and ruthless of the two. Sean was a manipulator. Whatever ploy he'd used to convince Donnie didn't matter now. That old saying rang like a bell in my throbbing head: *If it's the last thing I do, I'll find you both.*

Sean, that oily prick, had slipped the Beretta under my pillow before walking out the door and stealing my car. He left one bullet in the chamber but took the magazine. Maybe he thought I'd be so depressed I'd kill myself. I had other ideas about how to use that gun.

The phone rang. I picked it up and heard a voice identify itself as the front desk manager.

"Your friends left an envelope for you," he said. Then he added: "Checkout time is eleven o'clock."

At five minutes to eleven, muzzy-headed and with wobbly legs, I headed for the lobby to turn in the key. I suppressed a sour gas bubble rising from my gorge. The clerk handed me a plain envelope with my name on the front. I bought a copy of the *Times* on my way out sensing his eyes boring a hole in my back.

Out in the humid, smoggy air, I opened it. A pair of twenty-dollar bills fluttered out. Three lines in block letters: "Half beats a third. Better start running, mate."

Signed with a flourish, his "S" an ego-trip.

I cursed and put on my shades, glancing briefly at the headlines. Just below the fold, in caps: *Bomb Rips Sheriff's Evidence Locker*. The subheading was no comfort, either: *ATF investigates*. The photo showed crime-scene techs milling around the front of a cement-block building where a metal door tilted at a 45-degree angle. No mention of the missing topaz.

Maybe I had time...

Sean must have convinced Donnie to blow a big hole to

distract the cops. He wanted me on the run while he took off with my stone. I skimmed the rest of the article. I blamed myself for blindly trusting two men when I should have been picking up signs of the looming treachery. Sean was smooth, however. I had to give him that.

My radar on high alert now, Sean's warning to run meant something. Instead of calling a cab, I began a fast walk to the back of the L-shaped motel. An eight-foot wooden slat fence separated the property from a construction site where backhoes were clearing a lot. I'd just reached the top of the fence, straddled it like a lookout, and heard the four black-and-whites crunching the gravel of the parking lot as they turned in from the highway. Like a team of killer whales converging on a seal driven to the shoreline, they pulled up in a tight formation, running silent, feet from the door of the room I'd just vacated.

I didn't hang around to watch. I dropped to the dirt and was on my feet running fast. A foreman hollered something as I ran past his crew. Just then, I was too intent on putting as much distance as possible between me and L.A.'s finest.

I was waiting for them when they went through Customs at Suvarnabhumi Airport. I already had my driver paid off in the cabbie queue for their arrival from baggage.

My driver, as instructed, followed them to a third-rate hotel on the Khao San Road. Vendors and cliques of bar girls like sleek wolfpacks mobbed passing tourists, middle-aged men handed out advertisements for different bars along the street, and gaggles of vendors in their stalls sold every kind of cheap trinket from pornographic ashtrays to Viagra pills. People-watchers sat beside the road at outdoor tables beneath signs that listed Tiger, Singha, and Chang beers and diluted mixed drinks with oddly American-sounding names. Disco girls dressed like sailors or schoolgirls in pig tails gazed at the passing crowds eager to pluck a single hesitating male out of the herd and lead him off to a bar or a love hotel. Signs advertised various sex acts beneath a girl in an neon-yellow bikini dancing on a rotating platform. A hand-drawn sign advertised sex acts and prices in Thai, German, and English, one involved blowing smoke rings with a body part not meant for exhaling.

On their second night in Patpong, Donnie got drunk on his own. He had two women in miniskirts on each arm. From the way he stagger-walked, I knew he wasn't drawing many sober breaths. I followed ten feet behind. In that noisy street packed with locals and tourists from a dozen countries, I was invisible. I could have gotten close enough to tap him on the shoulder. The girls chattered away in Thai mixed with phrases of English, like "How long you here, cowboy? They held on to their "farong," as they call suckers they intend to bilk, and led him straight past an old lady in a sarong at the front of a love hotel, a scummy-looking flophouse you wouldn't put your dog in despite the fact they earn as much as those shell companies of my friend Gilberto.

The taller girl, more heavily made up, eyeballed her partner and stood back while she conducted the money transaction with an old lady wearing a long gray braid down the back of her sarong. Donnie was hustled by these pros so fast he barely knew what was happening. The taller girl made him understand "pay" with exaggerated gestures. When he drew out his wallet, she snatched it out of his hand with deft fingers, well-practiced in the art of hustling tourists.

Donnie was pushed ahead to a narrow stairwell as I watched from the street. They led him upstairs, one in front, one behind like a pair of handsome village girls leading a wounded ox out of a ditch.

In seconds, I was standing in front of the old lady with my own wallet out. I dropped three fifty-dollar bills onto the table. In baht, it was more money than she'd make in a month. She scooped the bills and they disappeared from sight. Thais smile more than any other people on the planet. I smiled and put my finger in front of my lips.

"Me surprise friend," I said and pointed at the stairs where the trio had ascended. I doubt she understood my English but she understood my money.

Up the stairs, past rooms where giggling, high-pitched Thai voices like songbirds mingled with slurred German, Spanish, and American grunts and monotones. Males up and down that grimy hallway were being given what they paid for even if they were too whiskey-limp to enjoy it.

I heard it, the accent of my boyhood; it came from a room at the end. Donnie said "Saturday" in his soft drawl—"Sa'erdee." The girls were still jollying him along, asking him the standard "How long you Bang-kok?" greeting shouted up and down the Patpong until dawn.

The doors were flimsy bamboo. I simply shoved it open with my hand. Donnie was lying in bed still dressed. The smaller girl was straddling his midriff bumping up and down, keeping him preoccupied while the taller girl—a ladyboy, I now recognized clearly—was holding his wallet with one hand and tucking bills into his cleavage with the other.

My metal-capped fish billy struck him in the forehead with a *thwock*. He dropped straight to the floor, the wallet falling free. When the girl on the bed swiveled her neck to see what was going on, I was already delivering the second blow. Her mouth opened to scream but the sound died in mid-shriek as the fish billy caught her in back of the head. She fell over Donnie's chest, her long, blue-black hair covering his face. They'd both have serious concussions when they woke, maybe brain damage, but at that moment, I didn't care.

Donnie, stupidly drunk, must have thought the other girl had jumped on the bed to join them. He didn't know what was happening until I shoved her limp body aside and he saw me.

"What the—holy *shee-yit*, Neill—is that you? What are you—?"

"Where's my stone, Donnie?"

He tried to get up, but I placed the filleting knife—my other purchase at the nightmarket—against his Adam's-apple and turned it so that he could feel its razor sharpness.

"Be quiet," I said, "I'm talking now. Where's my stone?"

"Sean...in the hotel. Christ, Neill, can I sit up?"

"Don't move or I'll slice your throat, you fucker."

"OK, OK, easy, Neill," Donnie said. "Sean said we could—"

"Shut up, you lying dog! My stone," I repeated. "Where is it?"

"Sean, he's selling it."

My stomach lurched. Too late. Then Donnie said, "Got us...buyer. In the morning."

I breathed again. I pressed the flat side of the blade

harder against his throat.

"Where...is...my...topaz?"

He gagged, then blurted out the one thing I needed to hear: "Iss...it's in the room behind...vent—"

"I'll ask only once. Where is Sean right now?"

"Nana."

It figured. The Nana Hotel's a legend in the Bangkok sex industry.

The billy came down on his head with a satisfying snap of the wrist. His eyes rolled up and his head fell back on the dingy pillow.

"So long, traitor," I said. "Hope you like rotten fish heads and spoiled rice."

He'd be eating a lot of it in a Thai prison when the police arrived. On my way past the old lady downstairs, I said, "Maniac...American...attacking girls!" I pointed backward toward the stairs. No smile this time.

My driver was waiting for me in the street. If I'd told him to run over his grandmother, he would have done it for the money I was paying him.

Hello, Sean, here I come...

He arrived back at his room at three in the morning, early for a Bangkok reveler. I knew he had a load on from the way he fumbled with the card key and his feet shuffled in front of the door.

As soon as the light went on, he saw me sitting cross-legged on his bed, hands folded in my lap. I'll give him credit. He took a sudden step backward and then composed himself.

"'lo, Neill," he said.

"Hello, Sean," I replied. "Remember this?"

I slowly lifted the Beretta from my lap and held it up. "Let's have it."

He thought about saying something clever, changed his mind, and took the topaz out of a fanny pack.

"Are you nuts?" I said. "You took that to the Nana and you still have it?"

Sean's a tough guy. He didn't object when I cuffed him. He merely asked if I was going to shoot him.

"No," I said, "you're a soldier. You understand how it's played, right?"

I pointed at the heap of towels in the corner. "You'll need those for later," I said.

Sean's vanity is where he lives. I wanted to hurt him there. I wondered how attractive women would find the aging playboy without his ears. My filleting knife took both off in neat slices. Sean screamed behind the gag. His eyes popped to the size of quarters when I aimed the blade at his crotch and made flicking motions. Fat drops of blood dripped from the blade. I pulled the gag down.

"Not that!"

I laughed. "I'm done with you, O'Reilly."

I took a final look back as I closed the door on him; he was rocking and moaning from the pain.

In Bangkok, where food has been preserved for centuries without refrigeration, you can find someone to do anything for you for a price. I found an old man setting up his fish stall on the Chao Phraya River before dawn. His face was crisscrossed with a thousand wrinkles and he had three teeth in his head. He took the ears from the bloody towel I'd wrapped them in, clucked at me as if I'd given him a couple figs. He wrapped them in banana leaves, salted them down, said something in Thai and handed my leaf-wrapped ears back to me.

Who says crime doesn't pay?

I have the money from the Temple Topaz, a villa near Playa del Carmen, a cook and a maid, and an ex-pat community of well-off Americans and Europeans to hang out with.

Before I left Thailand, I brought Sean's ears to a gold worker who fashioned medallions out of them. Thai gold is high in purity, 23 out of 24 carats. One is a good-luck Buddha amulet with a delicate filigree design around the circumference. On the back is an image of St. Nicholas, patron saint of thieves and the words: *Thank You.* The other I carry in my pocket because it's too heavy. It's a pendant of the Moirae, the Three Sisters of Fate with their names inscribed on the back: Lachesis, Atropos, and Clotho. They determine the fate of every mortal, God, and Titan, as my old college professor once said. Between these two medallions, I'm pretty sure I've got the curse covered.

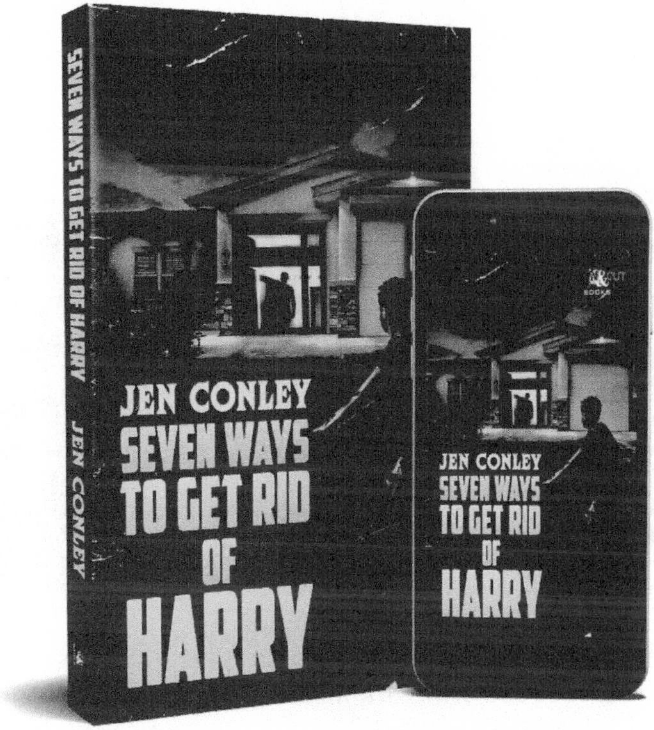

SEVEN FLUTES
Paul McCabe

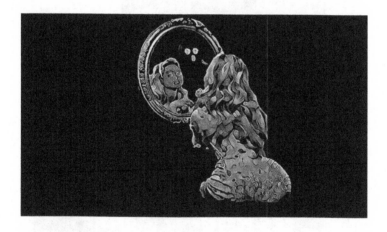

The flutes came after my brother died. Days after his illness finally took him away from us, I heard them for the first time, floating out over the dry hills toward our house.

I had been reading at the kitchen table, half-heartedly chewing a sandwich. Dad was upstairs, making so little noise that he could've been doing anything. His guitar was quiet, his T.V. too. There were no sounds in the house, no sounds around the house either; the entire countryside flying out from our small cottage was a still and silent valley, barren of everything but heather and turf.

But, when I was about to finish my sandwich and ask Dad if he wanted to go see a movie in Letterkenny, I heard the first few notes flitter through the open window like airy insects. Jumping notes. Notes that laughed and tinkled like fingers only lightly brushing a string or fixing a key.

I stood up and went over to the window and looked out. There was no one about, not a soul. The late afternoon sun was just slouching into early evening and the light was deepening, broadening, becoming a dense orange on the horizon, and in it I could see far out in all directions. If there was a source to the sound I would've seen it but there was nothing for miles.

"Dad!" I shouted up the stairs. "Dad, can you hear that?"

There was no reply but I heard a soft creak.

"Dad? Are you playing music?" I asked.

The sound still drifted about in the stale air of the house, scampering over the shelves and the bookcases, hollowing out the place even more than it had already been. Despite that, it was a pleasant sound. Airy, fizzy.

I walked up the stairs and thought the flutes were louder the further up I went. Not by much. But there was a definite clarity that became noticeable as I reached the landing, like a spotlight had fallen on the sound.

What a beautiful sound. The thought came from deep inside my chest, somewhere I didn't know. Somewhere dark. I thought I could distinguish it...different pitches...different notes—maybe different instruments. But it was all so dense, so layered together that it was all *one sound*, one scampering, flurrying wind of notes.

Dad's door was open but when I looked inside his room

was empty. There was still steam in the air from the shower he had taken a few minutes ago but the open window was quickly pulling it outside. There were clothes laid out on the bed and a pair of boots on the floor, all ready to be worn.

I heard another creak behind me.

There was a door at the far end of the hall. Beyond it was Danny's room, which we kept open. It was closed.

Just looking at it made a shiver cross my spine, something so quick that I barely noticed it. But I noticed the flutes get a little louder, a little *eager* even. They jerked around me, pushed into me from somewhere far off. For a second, they changed, grew harder, colder, like someone tickling piano keys with a set of sharpened steak knives.

"Dad?" I shouted again. I heard another creak from behind the door and started towards it, ignoring the sick feeling in my stomach. The flutes rose another pitch, got quick.

I laid my hand on the door and pushed, felt the wood hold back, just for a second, as if someone was pushing back at me, then release and swing open. As soon as the lock left the latch the flutes stopped. They blew away, out of the windows, the cracks in the wood, the edges of the doors. They didn't leave an echo behind. They were there one moment, rising in pitch, and then gone the next instant, as if they had been sucked out in a vacuum, leaving only a faint dryness in the air, a shallow flavour—the burnt taste of ozone. And a coldness that lingered.

My dad was sitting on my brother's bed wearing nothing but a towel, still damp from his shower. He looked round when the door opened, startled, as if he had been interrupted. He looked strangely undefined, like a watercolour painting.

He didn't say any words to me, just looked at me a moment before looking away, staring at nothing. But I got the message—his face said enough. Maybe I should have said something but I didn't. I just closed the door and turned around to go back downstairs, already forgetting the strange chiming flutes.

Later that night, Dad and I made a tasteless pasta Bolognese which we ate in silence in front of the T.V. BBC were showing a re-run of *Terminator*, one of my Dad's favourite films and one that he never failed to catch whenever it came on the small screen. It was already dark outside and a howling wind buffeted the windows.

Sarah Conner had just escaped the Terminator in the nightclub when there was a rap on our door. My Dad and I looked at each other expectantly.

"You heading out tonight?" he asked me, as he muted the T.V.

"No. Not tonight. I'm in for the night."

Dad got up and opened the door. From my position on the couch at the far end of the living room I couldn't see who was on the other side and, despite my Dad asking questions of them, I couldn't hear any voice in response. It was as if my Dad was talking to the wind.

"Who is it, Dad?" I asked. I waited for a reply but my Dad ignored me and, instead, talked in hushed whispers with whoever was at the door. From my angle I could only see his face and there crossed a strange, reverential look on it, just briefly, before it was flapped away.

I was about to get up and join him at the door when I suddenly heard those strange flutes again, heard them all the way down in my bones. Even softer than before but, somehow, more insistent, as if the player was playing with a shortness of breath. They made my toes curl. Dad seemed to hear them too for he looked as he had when I had found him on Danny's bed. There were tears pricking at the corners of his eyes...more than tears. Something wild jangled over his brow—a kind of strange grief that seemed to spread out over his entire face and turned his complexion waxy and his colour pale. His lips quivered like a guitar string and his brow knitted together into a furrow of deep crevasses. A shake crept into his shoulders that he couldn't stop.

I was about to go to him when a hand came out from behind the doorway. Small-palmed. Long-fingered. Thin-wristed. Old enough so that the paper-thin skin was loose on the bones and hung in places like rags would. It came up and rested softly on my Dad's shoulder, the fingers spreading out like the roots of a tree. It provided him with some comfort because I watched the shake in his shoulders begin to cease and his face clear of the stiffness that had crept into it like a cold creeps into an old house. The figure behind the door said nothing but her hand—I could tell it belonged to a woman—stayed fixed in place on his shoulder.

I got up from the couch and strolled to the door but as soon as I moved the still spell between us was broken. The withered hand withdrew in an instant and Dad closed the door quickly after it. The flutes too had disappeared.

"Who was that?" I asked.

"Just someone looking for Dunfanaghy," he replied, barely missing a beat. "They got lost outside Church Hill and they can't get any signal on their satnav."

"They're a long way from Dunfanaghy," I remarked.

"That's what I told them."

Dad moved past me again and sat back down and, as he passed, I caught the whiff of turf off him as if he had had his hands buried deep in the stuff. The smell lingered a little, cloying at him.

He switched the T.V. back on and the gunfire resumed. Sarah Conner and Kyle Reese where on the run once again, followed doggedly by the T-800 in a Semi-truck.

I walked over to the window by the hall and budged the blinds aside. It overlooked the front of the house, the driveway, the small vegetable patch, and the only road in to or out of the property. Even in the dark night I could see by the hollow light of the moon all the way to where the road disappeared in a bend in the hills and then on to Lough Beagh.

But I couldn't see whoever had come to the door. She had only left a moment ago. I should have been able to see her on the road, or among the dark hills.

But she was nowhere at all. She had disappeared.

I had a bad night, filled with strange dreams that seemed so vivid and frightening that when I woke in the morning my sheets were tossed to the floor.

I dreamt I kept waking up to the sounds of crying and moaning and whispering coming from somewhere in the house. The flutes were playing again, softly once more, but insistent enough that their vibrations rattled off under my skin and through my chest. I could hear them with every part of my body.

Several times I dreamt I woke up to those sounds. The moaning, the crying, the whispering, and the flutes all layered on top of one another like a cake until, after a while, they became indistinguishable from one another, all making one omnipresent, omnipotent noise.

I began to become afraid of the sound, afraid at how it seemed to push at me and hold me down in my bed like I was paralysed. The sound of the seven flutes—I could count them now—had turned into a heavy bass over speakers, metal scraping together, pressing me down into my bed.

I thought I could feel a storm rolling in, its thick banks of clouds blotting out the sky. I turned to look at the world beyond my window. Rain began to fall, peppering the glass, adding another pitter-patter noise to the growing movement.

My door opened and I was suddenly in Danny's room, standing by his bookcase and his dogeared collection of *Horrible Histories*. Dad was on the bed, Danny's bed, on his back with Danny's *Pokémon* sheets piled around his feet. On top of him, with her back to me, was a young woman with pale skin and long white hair. Her green dress was pulled up to her waist and her long, pale legs were covered in scratches and bruises.

The two of them moved sinuously together. The woman whispered things to my Dad, things I couldn't hear, things that made him smile with a kind of joy I hadn't seen on his face in a long time.

I was fixed to the spot by the bookcase by the flutes that were echoing so loudly in the small room that they made my eyes shake in their sockets. I wanted to screw myself shut but I couldn't. My chest felt like someone was crushing it.

The woman turned slightly on the bed and I saw the small gemstones of her pale breasts rising up to the flutes.

I felt a twist in my groin at the sight of her.

Then my heart clapped in fear.

Her face was contorted into a panic. Her eyes were so red, bloodshot, rimmed with tears so that the eyeballs themselves seemed ready to fall out. Her hand was clapped over her open mouth and, even though she was young, the hand was old and rotten. The hand from the doorway.

And she was wailing, screeching even, while Dad was inside her. And the screeches sounded like the flutes themselves, agonising tumults of windy notes ripping at each other.

The woman fixed her red eyes on me and the flutes reared back and whipped out.

I could feel her bony hands on me and the seven flutes howl.

Darkness came and a lockjaw silence.

Dad hadn't slept in Danny's bed. I checked as soon as I woke up. Danny's bed was untouched, as pristine as he had left it. His sheets were straight and his pillows fluffed, as if waiting for Danny to come back.

Just a dream. Just a weird fucking dream, one I never have to think about again.

Dad had slept in his own bed and that's where I found him, curled up under his sheets. But it was late and he usually got up early and had a couple of cups of coffee before starting the day.

"You alright, Dad?" I asked from the doorway. He stirred at the sound of my voice and turned to face me. He looked tired, as if he hadn't slept well either. There were heavy bags under his eyes and a slight redness to him like a picked scab.

"Yeah, I'm grand," he said as he got out of bed. He began to pull on a pair of jeans and a shirt. "Just don't feel the best. Put the kettle on would you? I'll be down in a minute."

I left to the kitchen and made him a strong cup of coffee.

I hadn't noticed the scratches on his shoulders.

Whatever was wrong with Dad lasted the next week and got progressively worse each day. He was getting headaches, pains in his joints, stomach cramps, sweats, chills, and nausea, all of which came and went at a moment's notice. By Tuesday he had lost his appetite. By Thursday he had been unable to go into work.

He refused to go the doctor and I didn't push him about it. I wasn't really worried and neither was he. We put it down to man flu. We both thought it would blow over in another day or so.

He went to bed early at night and locked his door. Several times I woke up to something, a feeling of someone in the house. I would walk about and check the windows and doors and find them all locked but that wouldn't satisfy me. I could always feel something around me, a silent something that would raise the heckles on my neck. Something wasn't sitting right in the house, something was off, like if someone drives your car and, even if they haven't changed anything, when you next sit in it there's something altered about it. Something you can't quite put your finger on.

I chalked it up to paranoia and the fact that I wasn't sleeping well which, in turn, stopped me from sleeping anyway. I told myself I was being an idiot but there was a new dimension to the house, a new undertone to the silence.

On Sunday I returned late from picking up another shift at the shop. I was dog tired and ready to fall asleep at the wheel when my car rolled in through the hills and pulled up outside the house.

It was only when I turned off my car and the headlamps cut out that I noticed it. All the lights in the house were off.

I got out of the car, unlocked the front door and stepped inside.

I had once been in a car accident on the M1. A van coming off the slip road went into the side of me and took us both into a couple bollards. There was an awful crash and screech of metal but, afterwards, there was the most perfect moment of silence. Absolute silence. Nothing seemed to be able to break it. The driver of the van and I looked at each other and found that we couldn't speak; the shock of the moment had robbed us, not only of our voices, but of any sound at all. The silence was a physical thing.

That was the first time I had ever heard a silence like that.

This was the second.

That same electricity hung in the air, filling the void that the absence of light and sound had created. Moving in it made me feel very strange, like I wasn't alone.

I flicked the switch for the landing light and could only barely hear the click before it was swallowed by the silence. No light appeared.

I wanted to call out but found my throat twisting around in protest. I steeled it and, in a loud voice, called out:

"Dad? You home?"

There was no answer. The words clacked off the walls and disappeared.

Asleep, I thought. He's asleep. He's been sleeping most days now anyway. And it's later than I thought it was. I'll check his room.

I was about to go upstairs when I saw something. Movement to my right.

Through the window of the kitchen I watched, nervous, as a figure moved across the hills several hundred metres away. Hunched—no, doubled over. Holding its stomach. It ran off kilter, almost drifting across the heath toward the small woods behind the house.

Far away as the figure was I could still recognise Dad. But I thought that he looked strange, swollen even. His stomach looked horribly distended. *What was wrong with him? What was he doing?*

I left the house again and looked out after him. He was almost at the treeline, almost beneath the shade of their branches and what little leaves they had left.

Then I heard them. The seven flutes. Back again. They came out from across the hills, hissing seductively from the direction of the woods. They seemed as clear as they had ever been, tinkling like wind chimes, fluttering like silk on a washing line, creeping into the earth like ice, worming into my skin, my muscles, my bones, hiding in the shallowest parts, filling the hollows.

That fucking noise.

I went on after Dad, calling to him over and over without any response. He ran on ahead of me, pulled into the dark copse. I hurried, sprinting awkwardly over the uneven ground, trying to stay on my feet amid the holes and the rocks. The flutes were getting more direct. They were coming from the within the dark of the trees.

Dad disappeared. One minute his stilted frame was leaning against a tree the next it was gone. I stopped on the edge of the wood. The white of his shirt was nowhere to be seen.

My heart was rattling loudly, shaking like a tambourine.

"Dad?"

There was a bustle of branches above me and a black cloud of birds burst forth from the trees and hurried off into the sky, their wings flapping in panic and their beaks squawking out in fear. I watched as they wheeled off into the night as one dense cinderblock of feathers before vanishing into a wave of dark clouds rolled in from nowhere.

I looked back at the trees and gulped down a thick ball in my throat. The woods beyond were closeted in a wall of shadows, penetrated only by the wispy, cackling noise of the seven flutes that seemed to worm their way through the dark.

"Dad," I said, "Dad, this isn't funny. Fuck sake, Dad, you're supposed to be sick!"

I got a response. Finally. The flutes stopped, just for a second, and I heard my Dad's voice call out, wailing in pain. Screaming in the trees.

I felt my balls tighten at the sound, retreat back up into me. My legs were already moving, heading off at speed into the woods, following the chewed-up track. I clambered over branches and tried to follow the screams. I shouted out to him, calling him, told him I was coming. I didn't know what was going on. My brain had stopped running—something was caught up in the gears. My legs just kept pumping on and on and my lungs kept on billowing air like a broken bellows. I could see nothing but trees all around me but they all looked the same. Soon I was off the path and struggling through bushes and brambles. The noise of the flutes called to me, crooking a finger in anticipation...*excitement*. I felt like my whole body was vibrating with sound—no part of me was still, everything was running at full tilt, bent toward the screaming and the flutes that echoed like hoarse laughs through the leafless trees.

I stopped and came across a small hollow between two mounds of earth and heard a final scream. The seven flutes stopped. Then came the same utter silence. I pushed through the bracken and found him, curled up in the hollow, covered in blood from the groin down. He was breathing so softly I could barely hear it and holding on tightly to something in his arms.

"Dad...Jesus, Dad," I said as I scrambled down into the hollow. He looked up at me as I approached with a serene look that went deep into his face. "What happened? Are you..."

I froze, seeing for the first time what he had in his arms. It moved slightly and made a small noise.

I knelt beside him and watched Dad whisper to the bundle. "What the fuck. *A baby*? Someone left a baby out here..."

Dad didn't reply except to lean forward and plant a gentle kiss on the wet head that peaked out from my his bloody *Depeche Mode* t-shirt. I had never seen him be so gentle. He held the baby with an awestruck wonder, looking down at it with eyes prickled with warm, proud tears.

I moved closer. "Come on, we need to get you to

hospital." I reached out to lift the two of them from the hollow and the baby twisted round to look at me. "We can bring the-"

No. Impossible.

Such blue eyes. Very blue eyes.

My mouth snapped open. The baby looked back up at me with its too big, too beautiful blue eyes. *Danny's* blue eyes. His blue eyes as they had been when he died at just seven years old. His blue eyes when we had closed his coffin.

Baby Danny, come back, with his baby blue eyes.

I didn't scream but I heard screaming. I looked up. Baby Danny cooed, but not like he used to, cooed different, hungry. Dad whispered something to him, some soft and fatherly words, and held him close. The wind whipped through the trees like the pants of some woodland god.

I looked up. At the top of the hollow, between the two mounds, was the woman. Her green dress was torn ragged. Her bare breasts were like moons. She was white against the black trees and she looked at me with those eyes worn red with unending rivers of tears. Angry. Sad. Vengeful. Mournful. She held her hand—her withered, desiccated rake—up clapped to her mouth but it did nothing. She was screaming, screaming at me, screaming at Dad, screaming at Danny…screaming so loud and so long that the screams turned to flutes that came for us all like scrabbling hands in the dark.

dillo

by
max sheridan

"The elements are all here: A memorable cast of characters wherein even the minor actors are given weight, a compelling and original road story, the precise amount of description to keep that southwestern sun bearing down on your shoulders at all times, and a fluid prose that allows the reader to turn the pages with the ease of an El Camino cruising across a battered American highway."

—Alec Cizak, author of *Down on the Street*

"A fresh voice taking on uncharted portions of the American literary landscape. Unique, funny, and wholly Max Sheridan's."

—Tom Pitts, author of *American Static*

"Pulpier than a box full of blood oranges, with the best, weirdest father/son road trip this side of a Waylon Jennings song."

—Joshua Corin, author of *Nuclear Winter Wonderland*

DON'T PANIC
J.D. Graves

I tell you it was awful. When I'd picked up Beulah yester-day morning, she looked fine. In typical Beulah fashion her shopping list was longer than her arm, while mine only had a few in's and out's. We stood in pet food load-ing our basket with cans of tuna when she suddenly turns to me, wide eyed, "When did we get a dollar store Deb-bie?"

I chuckled. I mean it was the silliest thing that woman had ever said and I'd known her forever. I said, "Beulah you know we've been coming here for three years now."

"Really for that long?" She sounded confused.

"Well yes," I said, "Are you feeling alright?"

She faltered a little as she reached for my shoulder. Then she muttered the scariest thing I'd ever heard, "Debbie, I think I'm having an out of body experience."

She's sixty-nine years old and drinks when no one's looking, so naturally I panicked, "Beulah you might wanna sit down!"

I knew it could be a stroke. I'd seen the signs years ago when Uncle Wally departed us that night at the County fair.

"I just don't feel like myself," she said, "I'm light headed."

God likes pranks. He don't allow you to leave with much dignity—at least not in Uncle Wally's case. He'd just bought Aunt Beulah a funnel cake when the good lord called him home.

"Can you tell me where you live Beulah?" I asked her.

"That's a silly question. In my house—the one Wally built with the white picket fence!"

It was worse than I'd imagined. Her clock was ticking. I swore she only had a few minutes left.

"Beulah!" I shouted, "You know very well that you haven't lived there in six months. Don't you remember your good for nothing Grandson, Bartlett, accidentally burnt it down!"

Some folks overheard me, but I'd already matriculated us down the aisle.

"He burned it down?" She asked more shocked than when it happened.

"You know we've been letting you stay in our garage apartment while my husband remodels it for you."

The poor dear's face became more distraught than Wally's the night he died. I mean his was covered in powdered sugar but...I wasn't about to let that happen to his better half near a stack of Meowmix.

I rushed her to the hospital immediately.

She protested the whole way there, but I knew I had no choice.

By the time I'd gotten her through triage, Beulah's family was on their way. Including that no good Bartlett. I mean—I didn't call him but he overheard my call to his mom and insisted on tagging along.

Beulah's people arrived. I pointed a shakey finger at the heart monitor, "Two hundred and twenty-two. That's stroke level!"

"Mah Gawd!" Bartlett said, with the dopeiest of dopey expressions across his mug, "Where is she now?" He asked this with such concern I was taken aback. Maybe I was wrong about good for nothing Bartlett. Maybe he really did care about someone other than himself.

A few minutes later we heard Beulah coming around a corner. She seemed in awfully good spirits for someone knocking at heaven's door. "I tell ya cutie! This is the silliest thing that's ever happened. Ain't nothing wrong with me!" Then she rounded the corner. The expression on her face reminded me of Christmas dinner. A sorta glass eyed smile full of holiday cheer. I thought, 'Dang this is bad if they've already started her morphine drip!' She saw us and sang out, "Heeeeeeeey! There's my faaaaaaaaaaammmmm-lllleeee! So good to see ya'll!"

Bartlett started snorting and laughing and I immediately knew I was right all along about that bastard. They wheeled her old bones into a room and he elbowed his way to her bedside. Beulah smiled wide at her grandson.

They held hands and looked deeply into one another's eyes.

Well, I had to remove myself from that weirdness. I was afraid I'd make sick all over the place when I remembered how Bartlett liked to play with matches. So I stepped outside with the doctor, this short mid eastern type with no hair.

"Has your Mother every smoked pot?" The doctor asked Beulah's daughter.

"What kinda question is that?" Before I knew it, I'd launched myself into a laundry list of Beulah's memberships and accomplishments. I mean how dare this foreigner accuse my Aunt of being some junkie!

"I only ask because—her urine test came back positive for Marijuana."

I nearly fell out.

I started to protest but her daughter got there before I could, "My mother would never...NEVER...*NEVER*—smoke drugs!"

I had to get away from that nonsense so I slipped back into Beulah's room, "Hey Beulah you'll never guess what—"

I stopped dead.

Bartlett sat her bedside. Her hand in his and whispered, "Everything's gonna be alright."

Beulah nodded intently, panic and fear on both their faces when they turned my way.

"I think she gonna be fine," Bartlett said, "I gotta get back to work now." And just like that—he was gone. Also gone was Beulah's holiday cheer.

I cautiously approached, "Beulah? Is there something you wanna tell me?"

She shook her head no. I asked again but added,

"because the doctor said you tested positive for—"

I didn't even need to finish before she started blubbering, "It was on my bucket list!"

I couldn't believe it and I told her as much, "The very idea a Sunday school teacher smoking Marijuana at her age!"

"I didn't smoke it. Bartlett brewed it in a tea last night and we drank it. Who ever heard of something not kicking in until eight hours later!" She started giggling, "I told him how disappointed it made me feel since I didn't feel nothing at all…until now." Her face fell, "Debbie, promise me you won't tell my daught—"

"Everyone knows—" I said flatly. "The doctor told everyone."

Beulah quieted, letting it all sink in. "If that's the case," she sighed, "you got any snacks?"

SINGLE SHOT

PRO 14

THE NEON GLARE

BY SCOTCH RUTHERFORD

A. B. PATTERSON

HARRY KENMARE, PI
AT YOUR SERVICE

YOU WILL BE VERY HAPPY HERE
Chris Fortunato

The canoe's passage over the dark water was as slow as if it were floating on glue. All three passengers had paddles— the woman in front with the short dark hair, the muscular man in the middle, and Peter Quigley in the stern, wearing khaki shorts, a khaki shirt, and an Australian bush hat. The two men had binoculars hanging from their necks, as bird watching had been the purported reason for their excursion up the river through the jungle with its spooky chittering and rustling and splashing.

Prescott James had introduced himself to Peter and Molly two days earlier at the little beachfront restaurant they liked to go to. He said he was just visiting Costa Rica and thinking of buying a place and he thought Peter and Molly looked like a couple of experienced ex-pats. After four months on the lam, Peter considered himself an experienced embezzler, paranoid and anxious, but not an experienced ex-pat, comfortable in the ways of a foreign culture. He certainly didn't like being in the position of explaining anything to anyone.

He had been annoyed at Molly for being excessively friendly and inviting the guy to go out with them today. He worried that even after four months of arriving in Costa Rica he still carried with him an aura of criminal intent. It was an attitude he was sure people picked up on, the alluring smell of five million dollars to be exact. Now here they were out in the jungle, and Prescott had made one too many glib assumptions about the wealth he assumed Peter possessed.

"I've had it, Prescott," Peter said to the man. "You ask too many questions. You're up to something, and I don't like it."

He pulled an M9 Beretta from his vest and pointed it at the man.

"Listen here," said the man in the middle, standing up at the sight of the pistol. "Any middle-aged guy down here in Costa Rica full time must have a good set-up. That's all I meant."

"Peter, no," Molly called from the front.

The brief distraction gave the muscular Prescott a chance to clip Peter in the jaw with his binoculars, sending him reeling back onto his seat. Then the muscular man executed an efficient dive into the terrifying water.

Peter fired the pistol into the depths.

"Peter, stop it," Molly cried. "You don't want to get into even more trouble."

But Peter wasn't to be swayed. He had escaped to Costa Rica with the funds from the international engineering firm he worked for. He wasn't about to let some guy hopped up on gin and tonics try to shake him down. The same thing happened a few months earlier when he was living on the Caribbean coastal town of Salsa Brava, where some guy out of nowhere said, "It must be good to be loaded in a beautiful place like this." He immediately moved to the Pacific town of Jaco. That was where he met Molly. She didn't mention anything about money to him, although she certainly knew where to find the most expensive restaurants.

She told him she had shot her abusive husband when they were struggling over a gun, and rather than go through protracted legal proceedings to exonerate herself, she had given up her job at the Nashville airport and fled to Costa Rica. Peter even checked it out on the internet and read all about the woman from Murfreesboro who had disappeared after questioning by the police.

It wasn't until after Molly had described the husband she had left in a pool of blood that he felt it only fair to share with her the story of his five-million-dollar embezzlement. He had been relieved to unburden himself.

"Where are you keeping the money?" she had asked.

"That I can't tell you. But at least we can have a good time."

Molly had presumed that Prescott was an innocent tourist and just wanted to go bird-watching with them. But Peter, who owned top-of-the-line German-made Zeiss binoculars, noticed that Prescott had a cheap pair he probably bought at a hardware store. In the world Peter had entered through his embezzlement, his senses had become heightened, and any glance his way or inference made to him about large quantities of money brought about hours of anguish and caused him to keep his Beretta clean and ready for action. In this world of high-finance robbery, it was eat or be eaten, and any evidence suggesting that someone was going to apprehend him or try to blackmail him into sharing the goods needed to be dealt with at once.

Peter remained standing in the canoe, aiming the Beretta at the still water.

"Where is he? He's been under water for at least thirty seconds now."

"Peter, don't shoot. This has gone too far."

Molly stood up in the canoe, making it shake and disturbing his line-of-fire.

"Sit down, Molly. I can't get a good shot."

Molly sat down. "You are making me nervous with that gun. You don't want to be shooting someone, especially in a foreign country."

"I didn't like that comment of his yesterday. 'We all have secrets.' He knows something, and I've got to take him out. Now, where is he? It's been forty-five seconds at least."

Just then, a figure in the distance emerged from the muck and began scrambling over the roots and vines at the shoreline. The parrots chirped, "Cheat, cheat, cheat" louder than ever.

Peter fired wildly at the shore, but once again Molly stood up, making the canoe rock from side to side.

"Stop it, Molly. I can't get off a good shot."

"He's gone now, Peter. Who knows where he went in that jungle."

Chris Fortunato

They paddled back hurriedly to where they had rented the canoe. They didn't say much on the way back into town, but Peter was upset. He had spent all this time laying low, and now some average Joe wanted to cash in on his hard work. That's why he carried the Beretta with him, to eliminate difficulties like this.

He turned to Molly as he pulled his car up in front of her hotel. "I'm packing my things and going up to Alajuela for a few weeks. I need to let things settle down. Who knows what this guy might do."

"That's a little extreme, Peter, but I'll try to understand," she added softly. "Am I invited?"

"Of course, you are," he said. "I don't want to go anywhere without you."

Ever since they had met, they had had a good time—boating, bird-watching, dining at lovely little restaurants along the shore, spending hours in his apartment watching movies, confident in the life of ease that lots of money brings. But Peter kept worrying that everyone saw embezzlement in his demeanor, and he worried that he wasn't enjoying life as he should be. One day at their favorite beach-side restaurant, he watched one of the old kitchen helpers sitting out in back with his plate of food and a bottle of beer listening to a soccer game on the radio. He wondered if that man might be happier than he was.

Back at his apartment building, a beautiful woman paced back and forth in the marble and polished-chrome lobby. In Peter's frenzy to have a good time, he had taken on a second girlfriend. If one girlfriend didn't make him happy, maybe two would. Right at this moment, with Melissa Urbe homing in on him with her blazing green

126

eyes, he knew that perhaps he had made a mistake.

"You're with that woman again. I don't like sharing, Peter."

Melissa was a free spirit surfer girl as colorful and as untethered as a quetzal in the jungle.

When Molly had taken off for ten days to see her sister who she said had flown in to San José with some personal items, Melissa had filled the gap. Peter knew he had grown lax in letting the relationship heat up so quickly. He couldn't help but be attracted when she had sauntered over to him at the Ribero Beach Bar and said, "Buy me a mojito, big boy?" He bought her one mojito and then another. After all, what was the point of taking that money if he wasn't going to have some fun.

How inconvenient to find her waiting for him right at this moment. "I'm sorry, Melissa, but I've got an important business meeting to go to."

"Oh, bunk," she said. "Does your important business meeting involve that woman?"

She tucked her hands into the front pockets of her jeans and pouted. With her tousled, sun-bleached hair, she was as elemental as something blown in with the tropical breeze. He wanted to take her upstairs and start proceedings with a nice, cold rum drink. She was the perfect antidote to Molly, who was steady and logical in all she did. He wanted both the impulsive and the controlled, and if it took two women to provide that to him, Peter had been self-indulgent enough to want that. After all, with a lot of money, you could buy nearly anything.

"I have to pack my bag for a few days, Melissa. I'll see you when I get back." He started toward the elevator.

"I wouldn't be sure of that," she said. "I might be with that German guy. You know, the one who walks up and down the beach with oil all over his body. I'm nobody's fool, Peter."

Melissa had a way of saying exactly what she thought, often telling him he acted like a clerk in a bank. She mentioned the brawny German to make him feel jealous. But he accepted her criticism because he knew he acted like a clerk in a bank. After all, as an international tax accountant, he had been a glorified clerk for that engineering firm. But Melissa had brought paddle boarding and impulsiveness into his life. She was exciting in ways that he had only fantasized about while spending years tallying global receipts for his fat-cat employers who profited from bloated municipal budgets and projects that dragged on for years.

"You don't know how to enjoy life, Peter. Really enjoy."

He asked, "Then why have you spent time with me?"

"Because you have money. I'm not ashamed to admit that. A man with money is a handsome man."

There it was again, the money issue. He couldn't enjoy his money without everyone wanting a cut of it.

"I'm sorry, Melissa, but I really have to go for a few days."

She turned and fled from the lobby out to the street.

Peter hurriedly packed some clothes, tucked some wads of money into the false bottom of his suitcase, and was ready to go.

In ten minutes, he pulled up in front of Molly's hotel, and she jumped in, throwing her designer knapsack onto the back seat.

"Off to Alajuela," he said. "We'll find a nice upscale place to hide out till everything calms down."

"Everything?" Molly inquired gently. "You've let one

incident cloud your whole attitude."

"Ever since I came here, I've been looking over my shoulder," he said. "I need some peace and quiet."

He sped along the long stretch of highway that cut through lush coffee plantations as they made their way to the highlands in the distance.

"You need to take a pill or something to calm down," Molly said. "Take a deep breath. Maybe we can go to a place with a spa and take a yoga class tomorrow."

"Sure, sure," he said hurriedly, his mind not on yoga but on the car behind him.

"Stay calm," she said soothingly as if placating a troubled adolescent.

"There's a light blue car behind us," he said. "Didn't you see it near your hotel when I picked you up?"

"There are hundreds of light blue cars in Costa Rica," Molly said. "And there hasn't been an exit for fifteen miles, so he has no choice but to be behind us."

"He could speed past."

"Peter, relax. You're reading the worst into every little thing."

Peter said nothing but gripped the wheel tighter. "Look up a five-star place in Alajuela or thereabouts."

Molly started tapping on the keypad of her phone. Finally, she said. "Here's a place, the Hacienda Altamaria. Very luxurious. First-class service. Farm to table."

"Book it," Peter said. "Get a suite. Tell them we're staying at least a week. I've got the money." He laughed, trying to force himself to relax. He had the money, all right.

Two hours later, they pulled up at the luxurious spa hotel in pale green stucco and a red tile roof in the verdant foothills of the Poás Volcano, staring down at them from a distance. The clean air, fragrant with the musk of the

129

rain forest detritus made Peter felt he finally could begin to enjoy life.

At Molly's urging, he took a hot shower and used her botanical soap and shampoo. As he emerged from the bathroom, he saw that she was all ready for cocktail hour, wearing a lovely flower-print dress. Her dark hair was brushed to a sheen.

"Feel better?" she asked.

"Considering that only rock stars can afford this place, it is less likely that a crackpot will be accosting me here." He wondered what had happened to that guy Prescott after clawing his way out of the swampy water. He thought of Melissa, too, but the problems she was causing him were in a different category, one of his own making entirely. Ultimately, she was no problem. He could buy her off.

"Come on, get dressed," Molly said. "Let's go down to the veranda and have a cocktail."

"Sounds swell," he said, trying to be upbeat, hoping a luxurious week would allay his anxieties.

A soft blue dusk had settled in over the mountains, and the waning light cast orange and mauve bolts across the sky and sparkled on the rich mahogany earth of the coffee plantation at their feet. Peter felt a comfort that had eluded him for the past six months. He and Molly sipped their coconut, passion fruit, and rum cocktails and stared out toward the sleeping volcano in the distance. The chattering of the jungle beyond the coffee plantation did not irritate Peter now, for it was now in a language he could not understand. He heard no accusing words from the dark unknown.

"This is why I came here," Peter said softly.

"It is the peace and quiet that only money can buy," she said.

He didn't want to contradict Molly at this moment, but it dawned on him that it was a peace and quiet that anyone could enjoy should they be here right now. During all those years grinding away for Breedlove and Jaspers Global Engineering and living alone in that apartment in that dead-as-death apartment complex, he had never given himself over to beautiful scenery or meeting enjoyable companions. Now, the moment he felt he should be relaxed, he found a reason not to be relaxed. He had come to realize that this fugitive life required far more work and far more introspection than he had ever experienced.

"Why Jim Teffington," a voice bellowed from the end of the veranda. "I'd know you anywhere."

Peter turned and saw a large man with a pint of beer in his hand striding across the veranda toward him. The man, with his red face and shock of white hair, possessed the spewing energy of an exploding volcano. He came to a halt in front of Peter.

"Second floor of Mr. Tate's house at Tabor Academy. Don't you remember me. Tom Boyle. Of course, I'm not the lean, mean halfback now that I've put on these pounds of USDA prime beef." With his free hand massaging his girth while he laughed, he stood in front of Peter and Molly like a dog waiting to be petted or fed or somehow mollified before it bit.

"Remember how we'd sneak in vodka and poor old Tate didn't know a thing. Of course, he was polluted himself on Friday nights." He coughed up a mirthless laugh, and pinned down Peter with the hard, wet eyes of a snake.

"I didn't go to Tabor, Mr. Boyle," Peter said quietly, regretting he left his Beretta in the suite.

"You didn't," Tom Boyle asked, stunned. "You sure?" He splashed his lips into his beer, aggrieved that

131

someone didn't fit into his memory.

"I am absolutely sure I wasn't there," Peter said firmly.

"Well, listen," Boyle began. Then he stopped, suddenly noticing Molly. "Ma'am, pleased to meet you."

Molly shook his hand listlessly.

The strange boisterous man in the untucked yellow shirt looked like he was about to shake hands with Peter, but he recoiled quickly as if in shock and said, "Oh, I must be mixing you up with that Teffington fellow." Then his voice grew somber, trembling with evangelical resonance. "You're that fellow whose picture I saw in the paper. The guy who ran off with five mil from that engineering firm. Wait till I tell Eleanor. I am standing in the presence of genius. You did what every red-blooded American boy wants to do. Grabbed the loot and high-tailed it to paradise." He shot another laugh into the wilderness.

"You are mistaken," Peter said as calmly as he could, casting a worried glance at Molly. Her solemn demeanor seemed to be urging him to maintain his composure. "I am the head greenskeeper at Fernbrook Country Club outside of Tuscon, Arizona. The only thing I run off with is abandoned golf balls from water hazards and only then so we can resell them at deep discount in the pro shop." One thing he had learned was that a falsehood, embellished with enough detail, became true, especially to those who seemed to be drinking too much.

"Well, I'll be," Boyle said, stepping back, staring into his beer as if interpreting a secret message in the dispersing foam. "Twice bitten, thrice shy, isn't that what they say? I'll bid you nice folks adieu. It must be this fine Costa Rican beer affecting me. They use all German equipment, I hear."

With that, he was gone, bounding across the veranda

and then into the lobby of the hacienda.

Peter turned to Molly. "He mentions German beer-making equipment, and earlier, I was talking about my German binoculars. And then there was that German guy on the beach all slathered up in oil. German, German, German. Is something happening here I don't know about?"

"Peter, you've taken your paranoia to an extreme. That's pure coincidence, like my girlfriend wearing the same color dress as I do when we have lunch." She stroked his arm. "You've got to relax. But, I can't help but ask, who is this German guy?"

Peter had recognized his mistake just as he was speaking. Melissa had mentioned the German guy, and he couldn't very well mention that to Molly. How could he have been so foolish to have let that slip? How many slips had there been that he didn't even recognize?

"Some guy on the beach the other day. He was looking at me strangely."

"And he was slathered in oil?" Molly said, smiling. "How did you know he was German."

"I heard him speaking to someone," Peter said, hoping to move away from the topic of his paranoia over German references. "I've lost my appetite. If you're hungry, we can order room service."

Back in their suite, Peter said, "It's time for me to find another country to live in. I need to get a false passport somehow. I should have planned this whole thing better, but taking the money was an impulsive thing."

"Sort of like suicide," Molly said.

He decided not to respond to that. As for the passport, she had a solution, and it involved her taking a picture of him with her phone. A contact she had back at the Nashville airport could fly his Learjet down to San José with the new passport, and then fly both of them directly to Corsica, where they could hide out in a hill town. As efficient as ever, she had it all worked out. Peter would have to wire half a million dollars from his account, which he now said was in the Caymans. After all, if he couldn't trust Molly, he was a goner. Getting away with crime was expensive, but Peter was willing to pay nearly any price to find peace from the threats all around him.

The next morning, he packed his bag with anticipation that he would find the happiness he had been looking for. Molly had ordered a car to pick them up and drive them to the airport in San José. Peter had no problem leaving his car behind to melt into the pavement at the Hacienda Altamaria.

"You're okay going to Corsica with me?" he asked.

"Sure," she said. "I'm in all the way as long as you're paying."

They waited under the hacienda's portico for a few minutes. Then a car pulled up.

"Here it is," Molly said.

"This is the light blue car that was following us yesterday," Peter said. "What's happening here?"

"I told you, half the cars in Costa Rica are light blue."

"That's not true, Molly." His anxiety was such that for the first time he was chafing at her certainty over everything. What made her such a know-it-all when before coming to Costa Rica all she did was work at the airport handling commercial tenant rentals? He was the man who had stolen five million dollars, after all. He was the genius people envied. He had to stand up for himself more.

"I guess I'm not right about everything," she said quietly, sensing his distress.

"Mr. Peter Quigley," a voice barked from right behind him.

Peter turned and saw the oafish man from yesterday. Today, the man wore a bright pink shirt. Before he could tell the man to go away, the man spoke again.

"U.S. Marshals Service. Please put your hands behind your back. You are under arrest. Good job, Nadine."

"Nadine?" Peter muttered, feeling like a child lost in the confusing world of adults.

The woman he knew as Molly stepped back and looked out toward the clamorous jungle as if meditating.

The man hustled him into the back seat of the light blue Volvo. The man who had called himself Prescott greeted him with a smile.

"I had a nice swim yesterday morning. Thanks for asking."

The words in Peter's head collided in his throat, and he was mute.

The woman driving the car turned to look at him. Melissa! "Hello, Peter. Look what happens when you don't hang out at the beach with a lady."

"Okay, let's get going," the man in the pink shirt said as he got into the front passenger seat.

"Where are you taking me?" Peter asked numbly. "How did the Marshals find me?"

The big man in the front seat man started to laugh, which brought on chuckles from the other two. "We're not Marshals, you fool. We were hired by the employers you ripped off."

Peter was now more frightened than if it really had been the Marshals who had apprehended him.

"Where are you taking me?"

The man turned and said, "We're giving you a choice.

We can fly you back to the States, and you spend fifteen years in a country club prison running seminars on accounting for your fellow thieves. Or we drop you off at the coffee plantation down the road here and you'll work with coffee beans for the next fifteen years. You'll be a different kind of bean counter." The three agents who had conspired to entrap him laughed at this.

"You will have no passport and no money, and your employers will simply know you as Mr. Hoss," the man in the front seat added.

"What's in it for you folks?" Peter asked.

"We're each a quarter million dollars richer," the man said.

"I can buy a new paddle board," Melissa said.

Prescott chimed in, "I can get new binoculars."

They all laughed again, and Peter sat silently, staring out the window at the lush greenery passing by on the roadside.

"Better hurry up with your decision," the big man said. "The coffee plantation is coming right up."

Peter considered the options and remembered the old restaurant worker sitting outside the kitchen eating his food, drinking a beer, and listening to the soccer game. He didn't know it at the time, but he was looking at himself. He could be happy, after all.

"I'll work on the coffee plantation," Peter said quietly.

The man demanded his wallet and passport, which Peter handed over. They were done with him now. He was no longer part of their big joke. They would move on, with all their wiles and trickery, to snare some other fool running from the over-heated environs of the corporate world with a bundle of illicit cash. Peter was Senor Hoss now.

The car turned down a narrow dirt road and after a

quarter of a mile came to a stop. The clear air seemed to shimmer in the blazing sun. The dust from the road piqued Peter's nostrils. The bugs chirruped and buzzed among themselves, and far off in the vegetation some primate or bird made a deep-throated howl that Peter hoped was not intended as a sign of blood-thirsty welcome.

"From now on, you are Senor Hoss," the man in the pink shirt told Peter once more.

I am Senor Hoss, Peter kept repeating to himself as he walked down the dirt road. He had been instructed to keep walking until a man came out to greet him. The man's name would be Senor Alvarez. Finally, a man with a broad smiling face emerged from a pathway in the vegetation, waved to Peter, and lifted his straw hat from his head.

The man spoke in English. "Let me show you around. You will be very happy here." Peter was relieved that the man didn't follow his smile with laughter.

"I am Senor Hoss," Peter said.

"Yes, I know," the man said gently. "Yes, I know."

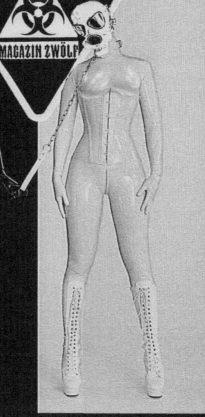

OF NOIR

SWITCHBLADE

JUNE 2020

MAGAZIN ZWÖLF

The Adventure
of the
Naked Guide

Conversation Pieces

Cynthia Ward

PROMOTES LITERACY
A Cheap Thrill
By: J.D. GRAVES
Just Another Job That Doesn't Pay Very Well
THRILL BOTTOM PRESS
DEEP EAST TEXAS

"**KRAJ** IS A HUMAN WRECKING BALL,
HIDING A TACTICAL MINDSET, ALONG
WITH HIS SENSE OF HUMOR."
—*SCOTCH RUTHERFORD,*
SWITCHBLADE MAGAZINE

KRAJ

STORIES

THE ENFORCER

RUSTY
BARN

A Cheap Thrill
By: J.D. GRAVES

The
LITTLE DEATH
of
JACOB GREEN

SWITCHBLADE

100 PROOF
MODERN NOIR

OUTLAW
SINCE 2017
WITHOUT LIMITS
TALES
POLITICALLY INCORRECT

SWITCHBLADE

QUICK & DIRTY
ANTHOLOGY
SHARP & DEADLY

OF NOIR
LOS ANGELES

THE WORLD'S **ONLY** NO-LIMIT
NOIR DIGEST MAGAZINE

ACCEPT NO SUSTITUTES

FOUR HUNDRED MILES OF
BAD ROAD

A Cheap Thrill By: J.D. GRAVES

EXPEDITION TO EDEN

J. MANFRED WEICHSEL

Time for your medicine.

Pulp Modern

Vol. 2 No. 5   Summer 2020

Andrew Bourelle • "Doc" Clancy • Timothy Friend
Adam S. Furman • Nils Gilbertson • Peter W.J. Hayes
Serena Jayne • Mandi Jourdan • Victoria Weisfeld

VICISSITUDE

A Cheap Thrill

By: J.D. GRAVES

TALL

PINES

LODGE

**A
NOIR
PLAY**

BY: J.D. GRAVES

CHEAP THRILL BIOGRAPHIES

DANIEL MARCUS has appeared in many genre and literary venues, including Asimov's, F&SF, Aeon, Skull, Witness, and ZYZZYVA. Some of these stories were collected in "Binding Energy," which Salon.com called "a cross between Raymond Carver and William Gibson." He is also the author of the novels *"Burn Rate"* and *"A Crack in Everything."* He has taught fiction at the UC Berkeley Extension and Gotham Writers' Workshop and was shortlisted for the John W. Campbell Award for Best New Writer.

PRESTON LANG is a writer from New York. He's published three crime novels, and his short stories have appeared in *Thuglit, Spinetingler*, and *Betty Fedora*.

SERENA JAYNE is a graduate of Seton Hill University's Writing Popular Fiction MFA Program. Her short fiction and poetry can be found in *Switchblade Magazine, the Drabble, Crack the Spine Literary Magazine, 101 Fiction, the Oddville Press*, and other publications. serenajayne.com.

JOHN KOJAK received his BA in English from The University of Texas. His short story "Don Pedro" appeared in *Beyond Imagination*, "American Hero" in *Down In The Dirt*, "Beauty and the Beast" in *Third Wednesday*,

"Happy Hands Cleaning Service" in *Bête Noire*, "Elizabeth Beatrice Moore" in *Pulp Modern*, "Shadow Rock" in *Eternal Haunted Summer's Winter Solstice* issue, "The Kobioshi Research Institute" in *Horror Sleaze Trash*, "The Archimedes Principle" in Cherry House Press's *Dreamscapes Anthology*, and "Going to California" in *Switchblade Magazine*. His poetry has also appeared in *Poetry Quarterly, Dual Coast, The Stray Branch, The Literary Commune, Dime Show Review, The Los Angeles Review of Los Angeles, Chronogram, Harbinger Asylum, The American Journal of Poetry, River Poets Journal*, and *Transcendent Zero Press's Epiphanies of Love Anthology*.

DONALD JACOB UITVLUGT lives on neither coast of the United States, but mostly in a haunted memory palace of his own design. His short fiction has appeared in numerous print and online venues, including Cirsova Magazine and the Flame Tree Publishing anthology Murder Mayhem. Donald strives to write what he calls "haiku fiction," stories that are small in scale but big in impact. If you enjoyed "The Night Jake Addison Saved the World," let him know at his blog http://haikufiction.blogspot.comor via Twitter: @haikufictiondju.

ROBB T. WHITE Born and raised in Northeastern Ohio, Robb White has published several crime, noir, and hardboiled novels as well as crime, horror, and mainstream stories in various magazines and anthologies under such pseudonyms as Robb T. White and Terry White. Nominated for a Derringer in 2019, his crime story "Inside Man" was selected for*Best American Mystery Stories 2019*. He has two hardboiled private eyes: Thomas Haftmann, featured in 4 novels and a collection of short stories, and Raimo

Jarvi (*Northtown Eclipse*,2018).*Murder, Mayhem & More*cited*When You Run with Wolves*asafinalist for its Top Ten Crime Books of 2018 and*Perfect Killer*for 2019. His latest work is the crime novella*Dead Cat Bounce*(2019). "If I Let You Get Me" was selected for the Bouchercon 2019 anthology and*The Russian Heist*(2019) selected by*Thriller Magazine*as its Best Novel winner for 2019.

PAUL McCABE is a writer living in Northern Ireland and has just completed his postgraduate degree in English, specializing on the work of H.P. Lovecraft, August Derleth and Robert Bloch. "The Danger of Common Men" was published in Belfast's 2015 *Papergirl* exhibition and another "I Stopped for Now" was published in*Grotesque Magazine* Volume 3, Issue 2.

CHRIS FORTUNATO has worked in book publishing for over thirty years, most notably, as an editor at Bantam Books. Currently he copyedits and proofreads for publishers. Stories of his have been published in *Thriller Magazine* and *Yellow Mama*.

J.D. GRAVES spearheaded the assemblage of all this mayhem. His stageplay, *TALL PINES LODGE* was an official selection of the 2016 New York International Fringe Festival. His other play *STANLEY AND JIM* played at the Manhattan Rep in 2009 to a total of two people. His short fiction can be found or is forthcoming in: *Pulp Modern: Tech Noir, Mystery Weekly Magazine, Black Mask 4, Switchblade Issue 3 and 4 and 8 and 11, Broadswords and Blasters 6, Tough Crime 1, Penultimate Peanut, The Door Is A Jar, Intrinsick 2.0, among others.*

He lives in the middle of the woods of East Texas with his wife and kids. Currently he's working on a novel and teaching. HE enjoyed feeding these salty words into this hungry machine.

COMING 2021

ECONO CLASH review

QUALITY CHEAP THRILLS

EDITED BY: J.D. GRAVES

Made in United States
North Haven, CT
23 January 2023

31445559R00104